MAR 2004

PHILLIPSBURG LIBRARY

6748 9100 140 096 4

**Praise for Guy Burt's**

"Akin to *The Blair Witch Project* . . . T̲
assured. . . . A story about that most ̲
being buried al̲
—*The New York Times* ̲

"An impressive and chilling debut."
—*Cosmopolitan*

"A frighteningly good plot . . . Expertly borrows the horror
and tension that made William Golding's *Lord of the Flies*
such a success."
—*MetroNews*

"Compulsively sinister."
—*The Times* (London)

"[A] compelling psychological tale . . . A quick and intriguing
book with a truly satisfying ending."
—*Publishers Weekly*

"The suspense and claustrophobia become almost
unbearable. . . . A remarkable debut by any standards."

D1445940

BY GUY BURT

The Hole

Sophie

The Dandelion Clock

# sophie

## Guy Burt

WITHDRAWN
Phillipsburg Free Public Library

PHILLIPSBURG LIBRARY
PHILLIPSBURG, N. J.

Ballantine Books • New York

YA BUR
Burt, Guy, 1972-
Sophie

A Ballantine Book
Published by The Random House Publishing Group

Copyright © 1994 by Guy Burt

All the characters in this book are fictitious and any resemblance to
actual persons, living or dead, is purely coincidental.

All rights reserved under International and Pan-American Copyright
Conventions. Published in the United States by The Random House
Publishing Group, a division of Random House, Inc., New York.
Originally published in Great Britain by Black Swan Books in 1994.

Ballantine and colophon are registered trademarks of Random House, Inc.

www.ballantinebooks.com

Library of Congress Control Number: 2003090143

ISBN: 0-345-44659-3

Manufactured in the United States of America

First American Edition: July 2003

2   4   6   8   10   9   7   5   3   1

# one

Matthew sits across from me on the boards of the empty room. His eyes are not on me at the moment. The side of my face hurts where he hit me. Outside, the sounds of the storm are loud; he keeps glancing at the windows as the plywood nailed up over them shudders and grates. We are in the kitchen of the old house. Shadows from the guttering candle flame dance and flare in the corners of the room, while the garden is torn and swept by the wind. The passages upstairs crick and murmur, as if they were alive with the walking memories of years.

I am breathing more calmly now. I am finding out where the boundaries are, beginning to know what rules we are following. He seems nervous, fidgety. I raise my hands awkwardly to rub the hair away from my face, and he sees the movement, turns his head.

"I'm sorry," he says. I don't know how to reply, so I say nothing.

He says, "Sophie? I'm sorry I hit you. I don't want to hurt you. But we have to stop the—you know, all the lies. We're past that now. No more games. All right?"

I nod, and he seems to relax a little. There is a splintering shriek as a branch pulls away from one of the trees outside, but he doesn't give any indication of having heard.

"There should be other things here," he says. "It feels like things are missing." I have no idea what he is talking about, but I nod anyway; it has become the easiest thing to do. I have no idea where this is leading, either. I shift my back against the wall, try to focus on the restless flame of the candle.

There is heavy tape around my wrists, but my ankles are free, and I have drawn up my legs so I can rest my arms on them. I am very afraid. He seems unsure of what to do next.

"The important things stay the same," he says.

"What?"

"Everything's changed. The house, the garden, the room. Everything's different." He sighs. "The important things stay the same, though. You. Me. You know." He smiles, and his face softens a little. He looks away.

When Sophie and I were young, our garden was large, stretching away from the side of the house, lined with flowerbeds and tall hedges. When the time of year was right, there were climbing roses and honeysuckle on the trellises. The ground was carved away in one place by a stream, and there were two wooden bridges over the water, leading to a muddy patch of land that had once been an orchard. Now, with only one or two of the original trees remaining, it was a place where the gardener made bonfires, and where the toolshed was. Crossing the stream, then, was to wrinkle your nose at the smell of old bonfire ash made wet. You had to step carefully on the soft ground.

From the house, there was only a small part of the garden which could easily be seen. Even from my bedroom, which was high up, there were places where the bushes and trees screened off the view. Because of this, and because there was so little for us to do in the house itself, Sophie and I made the garden our own. Our father was such a shadowy figure, and seen so rarely that he hardly impinged on our lives, while Mummy occupied the rooms on the ground floor of the house. She moved between drawing room and kitchen intermittently, going about her unfathomable business with a kind of measured precision that was both rather daunting and strangely reassuring. We knew where she would be, this way, and were able to judge our own movements to avoid her. At the time I am thinking of, I was five and Sophie was seven.

"This is going to be frogs," she said.

"What?"

"This is. This will be frogs. You know about tadpoles, don't you, Mattie?"

"Yes."

"That's frog spawn. First there's frog spawn, and then that turns into tadpoles. Then they turn into frogs. So this is going to be frogs." She touched a hemisphere of spawn that had protruded slightly from the surface of the water. "Isn't that strange?"

"I don't know. How do you know about frogs, Sophie?"

"I read it in a book. Isn't it strange, though? These little dots, they're going to become frogs one day." She stood up, abruptly tired of the conversation. "You could take some to school in a jar."

The gardener himself was a very tall, very thin man. His eyes were deeply sunk into the front of his head and he, rather like my mother, had his own pattern of movement. He spent the greater part of his time tending the garden where it adjoined the house, the beds near the driveway, the edge of the lawns. To keep the whole garden suitably trimmed and mown and pruned and weeded would not have been an impossible task, I think;

but the tall and silent gardener, in his heavy green coat and heavy brown trousers, was a lazy man. The farther back into the garden you went, the greater was the state of disrepair and decay. The day that we knelt by the stream and looked at the frog spawn, there was frost on the grass and, a few days earlier, the water in the furrows and puddles in the orchard had been crisply rimmed with ice.

Spring came grudgingly that year. There were late frosts for a long time, although no snow fell. The heating in my classroom at school had to be supplemented with a monstrous oil-filled convection heater. Its grimy beige paint was scabbed through in places, and it looked dangerously industrial among the drawings and the "Letters of the Alphabet" sequence pinned to the wall, as if it had the potential to do damage. I did take some of the frog spawn to school with me, just as Sophie had said. We put it carefully in a plastic aquarium on the nature-table. Almost all of it hatched out, and for weeks there were tadpoles to be seen in various stages of their development, before they became tiny frogs and had to be let go. Mrs. Colley was in charge of the junior school; she came into our classroom and was pleased by the tadpoles.

"Where did these come from, then?" she asked.

"Matthew brought them in, didn't you, Matthew?" Mrs. Jeffries replied.

"They come from frogs," I said. "The frogs lay the eggs, which is frog spawn. And then that turns into tadpoles and they turn into frogs. And it happens all over again."

"That's very good," Mrs. Colley said. "How did you find that out?"

"Sophie told me," I said. "She read it in a book."

"That's very good, dear," Mrs. Colley repeated absently.

The banks of the stream were freckled with the inch-long

frogs for a time, and then they were gone. The gardener took dead branches and the fallen leaves of the winter, and piled them high in the corner of the orchard. The cold weather and the rain had got into the bonfire, though, and it would not burn. The gardener walked away to his shed and returned after a time with a dusty grey can. He poured diesel over the heap, and set it alight. I expected the diesel to flare out and explode, but it didn't; rather, it burned steadily, with a strong smell. I watched as the gardener went back to his shed. He saw me looking, and an expression that was something like curiosity twitched in his face before he turned away. I ran off through the dead garden, looking for sticks.

Behind the wall at the far end of the garden stretched fields. They didn't belong to us, but to a farmer whose house and buildings were out of sight over a curve in the land. There was a scattering of trees that grew denser towards the top of a low hill. If you followed the trees, you found yourself walking along the boundary between two fields, where in summer the crickets buzzed and whirred around your ankles as you walked. Just over the skyline, the trees thickened briefly before the ground dropped away into an abandoned quarry. In the shattered rocks at the foot of the quarry walls there were little twisted shells and patterns in the stone. Again, like the garden, the quarry was a place where no one else came, and so Sophie and I went there often when the weather was warm.

March sunlight cut in sharp angles across the classroom.

"All right, children," Mrs. Jeffries said. "Put your maths books away and get changed for games. Susan, will you collect up the rods for me? Thank you. Matthew, if you find your reading book, you can sit and read until tea."

The rest of the class trotted happily out into the exhilarating air of the playground.

Throughout childhood, the muddled clutter that clumps itself around most children seemed to have eluded me. It happened not in some clearly defined manner, but instead there were a multitude of smaller things which conspired to keep a small, but noticeable, gap between me and my peers. Some children are afflicted by prodigious intellect, or comical obtuseness, or a remarkable ability or inability at art or sport. Mattie Howard, though, was never really any of these. Instead, I simply found that while I was accepted readily enough at school—even despite not being able to join in games lessons—I nevertheless sloughed off all the trappings of school as soon as I ran out through the gates at the end of the day. It was not, I think, my decision; nor the decision of my friends in class. At that age, a structure of politics exists among parents from which my mother was almost universally excluded. And so, where another child might have been setting off for a friend's house, or to a birthday party, Sophie and I were instead quite content to shout our good-byes and walk home together. For me, this was simply the way of things. The walk home was a fair length, and if there was no reason to hurry we might talk about what we had done that day, or what we had planned for the weekend or the evening. My five-year-old's achievements were trivial enough, but Sophie would have learnt astonishing and wonderful things; and these she told me, interspersed with her own questions and conjectures on whatever subject she had chosen. And again, this was simply the way of things.

One evening, after we had washed and done our teeth, Sophie wandered into my room and sat down on the end of the bed.

"Mattie?"

"Hm?"

She frowned. "What do you know about babies?"

"What do you mean?"

"Mummy's going to have a baby."

"Is she? When?"

"I don't know. Not yet."

"How do you know?"

"She told me." Interested, I sat up against the pillows. "What's it called?"

"I don't know. It hasn't been born yet. So? What do you think?"

I didn't understand. "Think what?"

She breathed out sharply. "It will be another person in our family. Do you see? Someone else. Younger than us."

"Oh."

"I mean, would you like that? Having another brother or sister?"

I thought about it. "I don't know, Sophie . . ."

"You *never* know," she said affectionately. "Everyone has to think for you, that's your trouble."

"I think I'd like it," I said. "Yes. I'm glad."

There was a long pause. Then she said, "That's good, Mattie . . . We can play with the baby, perhaps, when it comes. You know. Push its pram and things."

"That would be nice."

"OK. Go to sleep, now. Don't forget your 'haler."

"Night-night," I called after her as she left, and heard the whispered reply before her door opened, and clicked shut, comfortably close down the corridor.

That night, I had the nightmare again for the first time in weeks. It was the same as before; it was always the same. The jumbly, rustling shape of Ol' Grady slipped in through the door, sidling along, always keeping to the wall. The moonlight lit on its long arms and on the blank place where its face should have been. It was carrying something, but before I could see what it was, I awoke. Any sound that I might have made was crushed in my throat. It was a long while before I got back to sleep.

I shift position slightly, and the floor under me creaks. The walls of the kitchen are white-painted plaster, hard against my spine, and there are patches of damp showing here and there. Matthew has stood up, started to pace the length of the room in front of me. From some of the things he has said, I know he is thinking now about the nightmares. I know about them, of course, but I don't know what to say. My face aches, and I am constantly aware that each time I speak, I put myself at risk. At the same time, though, I think it is better to keep him talking for as long as possible. In the silence, or when he is letting out fragments of the past, I am thinking; trying to make sense of what is happening.

I say, "Do you remember when they started? The dreams?"

He looks round at me, surprised. "No, not really. They were always there. There was only the one, though. It still—I still have it. Sometimes."

"I know," I say quietly. He doesn't appear to notice.

"I never found out how you killed him," he says, and I feel a flood of apprehension.

"What?"

"Ol' Grady. You must have killed him before I was old enough to remember properly, because I've only got the dreams left." He laughs softly. "I remember you showing me what was left of him. But I've wondered for a long time now how you managed it. You could only have been five." He looks at me, expectantly.

"I don't really know," I say.

"Oh." He sounds disappointed. I concentrate on the dull throbbing over my cheekbone, and after a time he turns away again.

The sounds of the storm outside come and go. It seems like years ago that he dragged me in here, into this deserted house, past the chaos of the front garden. Rain and wind ripped through the long grass, tearing our faces, half blinding us. Even the memory of the rain seems now as if it came from another world, and while we sit here there is only the sound of it left. Every so often, the cracks around the window boards flare white as lightning strikes somewhere in the woods behind the house. The back of my shoulder itches but, because of the tape, I cannot reach to scratch it; the best I can manage is to rub myself against the wall.

He notices. "Sorry, Sophie. But I know you too well, remember?"

I shrug. "I suppose you do what you have to do."

"Right!" He nods, suddenly excited. "You do understand."

I blink, keeping silent. The words meant nothing, and it is unnerving to see his reaction.

Part of me is aware that my own calm, right now, is probably unnatural, an exhaustion washing over me in the wake of my earlier panic. Whatever its origins, I try to use it. When he talks—almost to himself, at times—I listen. When he makes no sense, I try to store the words in my head, to slot them into place later. When he says things that I understand, I try to add more detail to the picture I have of him. This is all I can do at the moment. I am afraid that it is not going to be enough.

I saw more of Sophie than anyone else, child or adult, and so I was wise to her ways and her habits. Where another person, a stranger, might have found some of Sophie's behaviour strange—and certainly precocious—it never occurred to me that this was anything other than, as before, simply the way of things. So it was only natural that Sophie spoke differently, used a separate set of words, when she was alone with me. When at school, or with adults, I would sometimes grow frustrated with her, because she seemed so stupid; she would be unable to answer questions to which she had told me the answers years before, and would sometimes appear to have trouble finding the right word to use (and I knew she was pretending). It was annoying, at times, but when I questioned her about this, wanted to know what she was doing, she would only say that it was a game.

"It's not a very funny game," I said once.

"It's not that sort of game, Mattie. It's like—it's a skive, you know? Like pretending to be clumsy so you aren't asked to do the washing up."

"How does it work?" I asked, rather intrigued by this.

"Well—in class, let's suppose, if the teacher wants you to answer a question, and you know the answer, what would you do?"

"Put my hand up."

"And tell her. Right?"

"Yes."

"But if you do that, you'll be asked more and more. Who's the cleverest person in your class?"

"Robert. He always finishes first, and gets the most stars."

"OK. But I expect that Mrs. Jeffries asks Robert more questions than she asks you?"

"Sometimes. And he has to do more of the workbooks, because he finishes first," I said proudly, beginning to see the point that she was making.

"All right. So it would be easier to pretend not to know—just sometimes—so that people don't take too much notice of you. Then you don't have to work too hard, but you still do OK—you don't come bottom in class or anything like that. Do you understand?"

"Yes!" I said, excited. "That's really clever, Sophie."

"It just makes sense. Teachers go very strange if you're good at something. You know that girl who's really good at maths—the one in the fifth form? She always has to sit in at break and do work, and they're all talking about scholarships to her next school and so on. It's a lot of bother."

"Is that what you're really good at?"

"I'm OK at maths. I've seen the books that the third form are using. I'm good at most things."

"You're really lucky," I said. "I'd like to be good at everything. Then I wouldn't have to do any work."

She sighed. "Oh, Mattie," she said, and cuddled me tightly. "That's what I've been *saying*. If you were good at everything, you'd have to do far more work than you do now. . . ."

But this seemed silly, and I decided that she was making another one of her strange jokes, and forgot about it for a time. It was only after many years, when I had managed to achieve some degree of objectivity in relation to the memories of that earlier childhood, that I was startled to realize the elaborate deceit that Sophie practised in order to avoid detection as being "good at everything." At seven years old, she had a more advanced and more subtle grasp of the nature and restrictions of intelligence than many adults. She also had a clear awareness of her own individuality, most especially in comparison with other children her own age.

And I, living in the shadow cast by a sun occluded of its own accord, hardly noticed at all—and what I did notice was a slender fraction of the reality. When Sophie came to take her entrance examination to her secondary school—which she did at age twelve, due to the somewhat unusual structure of our prep school, which accepted children of both sexes—she had to take an IQ test. For some reason this, far more than the prospect of the other impending exams, worried her; I assumed because she had never sat such a test before, and was unsure of what to expect. Several weeks before the exam was due, she bought a number of books designed to test your IQ at home, and went through them carefully, studying. She also completed the tests given in the books, marking her answers and tabulating her results. Many children—the more perceptive, anyway—know the trick of learning what to expect in IQ tests, and manage to bolster their results by as much as five or ten points. By the time the date of the actual exam arrived, Sophie had managed to maintain a steady result of around 125; bright, but not fiercely intelligent; in the top ten percent of the country, by average, but not in the top five. She was a solid enough candidate, considering the quality of her other papers, and the school was happy to take her.

I was ten at that time, of course. I looked through the spent and scribbled-on IQ books that Sophie had thrown away. It had taken her six or seven attempts before her results became constant, and she could accurately and consistently predict a score of 125; the last three tests all scored between 120 and 130. But the first test that she had completed, before she began to check her answers and learn what to do, indicated an IQ in excess of 180. The chart in the book didn't go any further.

The spring began to make itself known in our school playground, and there was colour for the first time in the flowerbeds and window boxes. The earliest manifestation of the new year had been the frog spawn, but now—making up for lost time, it seemed—there was life and growth everywhere. The trees on the hill behind our house cracked open with green, and the air began to lose the sting of winter, and become heady with the smells of leaf mold and sap from the sticky-buds in the lane. It became more reasonable to spend time out of doors, and Sophie and I availed ourselves of the chance to do so. It often appears to me, looking back, that I lived a huge part of my childhood outside.

Even the gardener acquired a newfound animation with the arrival of spring. Abandoning the seclusion of his shed in the orchard for greater and greater stretches of time, he moved about the garden as if on a predetermined path, from bush to shrub to sapling, carrying the instruments of his trade with him. Shyly, I stood and watched him when I could, for the gardener fascinated me in a way that no other adult ever had. He reminded me, more than anything, of the people and animals in *Alice in Wonderland*, which Sophie had read to me. I saw in his movements through the garden no kind of order at all; almost as if the reasons for what he was doing had been long forgotten. With two bits of board he gathered together the raked piles of leaves and put them in the wheelbarrow, ready to be taken over the stream to the bonfire. The places near the house began to look neat and well-tended, while the periphery of the garden remained chaotic and tangled as ever. My mother, who hardly ever set foot outside the house, never realized this.

One day, when Sophie was in her room doing homework and I was kneeling by the edge of the stream, watching the small fishes shoot back and forth under the water, the gardener came over to me. He walked awkwardly, as if not quite sure that he wanted to come close, and stopped a few yards off. We looked at one another in silence. From where I knelt, the gardener was outlined against the grey sky, his thin face hawk-like. He reached into one of the enormous pockets in his old brown coat and took out something fist-sized.

He held it out to me, not meeting my eyes. Excited, I took the thing from him carefully. It turned out to be a toad, cool in my cupped hands, and still sleepy from its winter rest.

"Thanks," I said, genuinely pleased. The gardener jerked his head up once, a sort of backward nod, and tramped off along the bank of the stream, his boots leaving regular impressions in the soft earth. I held the toad, studying its humourous face and wonderful eyes, which were hard and crystalline, as if they were made of tiny shards of broken glass, and a golden colour of great clarity and beauty. The toad opened and closed its mouth thoughtfully, and pawed at my thumb gently with one arm. It didn't appear to be in any hurry to go anywhere. After a little while, it peed on me. Enchanted, I ran to the house to share my toad with Sophie.

Unlike many girls, Sophie had no squeamishness for frogs or toads. She looked the toad over with appreciation. "He's lovely," she said. "Where did you find him?"

"In the garden," I said. "By the stream."

"He needs a home," Sophie said. "Find a box or something and put some grass and soil in it for him to burrow in. Toads like to burrow."

"And I like toads," I declared. "This one's a brown toad."

Sophie wasn't really listening. "If you like toads, there's a good story I'll read you," she said. "We could start it this evening. And there are lots of other animals in it as well."

"Yes," I agreed. "I'll go and find the toad a house."

My mother was in the drawing room. The standard-lamp by her chair was lit, and she was sitting, reading a magazine. I knocked on the half-open door with my free hand.

"Come in," she said. I took off my shoes and crossed the carpet in my socks, feeling the lovely warmth of the pile through my toes.

"Mummy, may I please have a box to make a house with?"

She looked at me carefully. "Houses are girls' toys, Matthew."

I was too excited by the toad to think properly before answering. "Oh, this one's not," I said happily.

There was a long silence, and I knew at once that I had done something wrong. However hard I thought, I couldn't see what it was.

"Don't contradict me," she said. I was suddenly frightened; the shadow of that shuffling, crumpled thing seeming to move over me for a moment. I blinked. "Do you hear?"

"Yes, Mummy," I said. "I'm sorry." I turned to leave; there were boxes in the kitchen, I thought, and no one would notice if I took one of those. But it was too late.

"What have you got there?" she demanded.

"Nothing," I mumbled.

"What? Speak sense, for heaven's sake. What are you holding?"

"It's a toad," I said, and held the toad out for her to see.

There was a pause while my mother observed the toad. Then, "Take it outside, Matthew, and get rid of it." I must have looked distraught, because she added, in a different voice, "It wouldn't like living indoors in any case, Matthew. It would most probably die, which would be upsetting for everyone. Let it go in the garden."

And then she sank back into her chair an almost imperceptible distance, indicating that the matter was closed. I nodded, and left, collecting my shoes at the door.

"What did you think?" I ask.

"I don't know. I don't think I thought anything. I didn't hate her, if that's what you're asking. There wasn't anything else. You get used to what's around you.

"It was just the way of things?"

He gives a start. "Yes." His eyes narrow for a second as he looks at me, and then he relaxes. "I began hating her much later. Because—because of a lot of things."

I fix my eyes on a neutral area of the floor and say nothing.

# two

The day was bright, with the fresh clarity of late spring. There was birdsong as we picked our way up the hill, the craggy stone wall to our right. There was a path worn through the field's edge here, and flat, smooth stones as big as plates and cartwheels nosed out of the packed earth under our feet. Sophie covered the ground easily, sometimes stretching her arms out as if she were balanced on a high wire, sometimes pointing things out to me as I followed behind her. At the base of the wall grew clumps and scatterings of wildflowers, and some of these Sophie would pick, slowly building up a colourful bunch as we proceeded.

I was somewhat out of breath by the time we had crested the hill. The newly green trees, their leaves still crumpled from being buds, heralded the lip of the quarry, and we drew nearer with excitement. The quarry was icy and too far away to walk to comfortably in the winter, and so for a few months we had not seen it—had, in fact, confined ourselves to the garden and the lanes around the house, and the village. The forced proximity with my mother was uncomfortable enough on its own, but there was also a separate, almost tangible, sense of being constrained. Sophie had told me halfway through that week that, on Saturday, we would go to the quarry again, and I had been in a state of eager anticipation ever since.

The fence around the rim of the quarry was very old. It had been made of wooden slats at first, but when these had become silvery-grey with age, and started to fall apart, someone had interlaced the slats with wire—mostly wide-meshed fencing wire, but also some barbed wire along the top. The whole effort gave the impression of having been made without conviction, and the faded warning signs had not been replaced or repainted since I was born. It was with only a little effort that we could scramble around to a convenient gap. The quarry itself was fairly shallow on three sides, with a steeper fourth side where the cages were. Turning our feet sideways on, and shuffling rapidly downhill, Sophie and I traced a path down the scree and out onto the quarry floor.

We examined it carefully.

"There's been some rocks down, over there," I said, pointing.

"It's not surprising," Sophie said. "Winter weather does that sort of thing. The rocks freeze up in the cold, and then crack and fall down."

I wasn't interested. "Let's look for shells."

Sophie nodded. "Right. Go and see if the bag is still there."

With a delicious sense of adventure building inside me, I trotted off across the wide expanse of strewn rock, heading for the cages. There was always something dangerous, and therefore exciting, about retrieving the bag at the beginning of a quarry afternoon. To do so meant to scramble up the loose rock at the foot of the steeper wall, and to get right up close to the mouth of the nearest cage. The cages were, in fact, more like caves with doors; deep holes extending horizontally into the rock face, and set with huge iron bars to stop people going in. The floor just inside, where you could still see it, was littered with ancient cans, brown with rust, their nature unidentifiable. There was a smell at the mouth of a cage that was something of damp, but more something else entirely.

The bag was there; I snatched it up, and hurried back to where Sophie was standing, my heart pounding, grinning like mad.

"There!"

Sophie took out the hammer, and we found a rock large enough to use as a crude, knee-high table.

"You can start looking for good rocks, now," she said. "Pick the ones with shells on the outside, OK?"

"OK," I said, and began searching among the debris.

Also in the bag, of course, was the large biscuit tin in which Sophie kept her books. While I was crouched down, turning over lumps of rock, Sophie would amuse herself by writing in her books, sometimes just a little of her funny scrawl, sometimes pages at a go. She wasn't really writing, though: I was old enough to know enough of reading and writing for myself to see that Sophie's Biro was scribbling gibberish, not real letters and words. But then, many of the things Sophie did were strange. She had been writing in the quarry books for as long as I could remember.

"What are they for?" I asked her once.

"It's a bit like a diary," she said.

"What do you write down?"

"Oh, lots of things. You know what a diary's like, Mattie. You tell what's happened to you that day, who you saw and what you did. It's like writing a letter to someone, except you never send it."

"Why do you do it, then?"

She smiled. "So that you've at least told *yourself*, you see?"

I didn't see. More interesting than Sophie's quarry books were the other things in the bag, the funnily shaped hammer with one flat end and one long, chisel-like end, for chipping and splitting rocks; the selection of chisels for use when the hammer alone was inadequate; the old screwdrivers, for scraping away the rock on delicate shells. It was mostly shells that I found in the quarry, and mostly one sort: round, curved ones, as large as Sophie's thumbnail. Very occasionally, there were other sorts of shell, spiral shapes and roundels that were larger and far more impressive than the common ones. I was intrigued beyond measure by the shells—the way that they were seated so deeply in the rock. Sophie explained that they were shells from sea creatures, and that the quarry was a seabed from many years ago. It was obviously just a story, but it was such a strange and splendid story that I adopted it at once as truth. But I never found any fishes in the rock, no matter how hard and long I looked.

Sitting on the quarry floor, the sky was outlined with the branches of trees. Everything else was bleakly empty, with only the cages (at the one end) and some tufts of scraggy weeds (at the other) to suggest that you were anywhere other than a different planet.

I look back at myself now, and it is only an understanding of Sophie's astonishing mind that prevents me from feeling a kind of contempt for myself. Sophie never lied to me. To other people, yes; and with measured and assured conviction, and she was never caught. But everything she told me was true. As I grew older, and gained some knowledge through my own schooling, and through dealings with others, I realized that some of the childhood fables I had grown up with—the fossil seabed on the hill behind our house, for example—were not fables at all, but plain fact. Sophie always told me the truth. But it was only very much later that I began to see that, if the most part of something is truth, then it follows simply that the remainder is likely to be as well. And so it was only very much later that I went back to the cages, on a foul and darkening day, with drizzle drifting across the empty quarry and the sky as bleak and bare as rock, to find out the truth.

He sits staring at the floor, his hands clenched together. His posture, opposite me, mimics mine, and his breathing is harsh like mine was earlier. After a while, he looks up.

"I didn't believe you enough," he says simply.

"When?"

"At any time. It doesn't matter. Perhaps if I'd known enough to believe you, we—"

"We wouldn't be here now?" I wonder if the words are safe.

He nods. "Not like this. Perhaps we *would* be here now, but—not like this."

"Is that the only thing you'd change?"

He looks up, and there is a curious respect in his eyes; something I hadn't thought I would see. "No. Hardly."

"What else, then?"

His expression hardens. "Don't push me, OK?"

I lower my eyes. "OK. Sorry."

I wonder how long this has been in his mind, this confrontation with the past. I have begun to understand what I am caught up in, but despite the comprehension I still find it almost impossible to believe that we are sitting here talking through events that happened almost twenty years ago. The candle flame shifts, fluttering like a tongue. The corners of the room, I have seen, are littered with waxy stubs. Outside, the storm comes and goes. He must have been prepared for this night for some time.

"Sophie?"

I look up, startled.

"What would you change?"

I almost smile; the question begs an obvious response. Instead,

I concentrate, scared that this is another test, not knowing what happens if I fail.

"I—I don't know."

"Oh, come on," he says, annoyed. "You can do better than that."

"I think I'd tell you more," I say, letting the words out slowly, watching all the time to catch a glimpse of the wrong reaction from him. There's nothing. "I think—I mean, you seem to know everything now in any case. Don't you?"

"I know *what* happened. I just don't know *why*. Why did you do it?"

"Do what?" I ask. A look of confusion crosses his face.

"Oh, all the things you did," he says vaguely, and looks away. I say nothing, wary of the fact that I seem to have come near to something very dangerous.

The holly bush was a favourite place of mine. Set well back in the less tended regions of the garden, it was in reality more of a tree than a bush; the sagging lower branches, however, had drooped to the earth and rooted there. There was thus formed a sort of teepee-like hollow in the centre of the spiky foliage, as high at its centre as the lowest branches stemming from the trunk, into which a determined child could scramble through a less dense patch at one side. This entrance was itself screened from view by a scraggy privet hedge, and the whole hideout en-sured a privacy that was implicit, but not actually guaranteed, in the rest of the garden.

Sophie, using an old tent from one of the sheds, and my help, had lined the holly bush with canvas, making it thoroughly waterproof under most normal conditions. The floor was cov-ered as well, and it was lit by candlelight. The execution of this project took us a full fortnight during the summer, working every afternoon; the results, however, justified the time spent. Completely secluded, the holly bush was perfect in its isolation. I dearly wanted to spend a night in it, but there was no chance of that. The thick smell of the old canvas greeted you as you pushed your way under the heavy swatch of holly branches, and as the chamber inside filled with the hot smell of candles you could easily imagine yourself to be anywhere in the world. Sophie and I would sit with our backs to the central trunk, our legs pointing to the edges of the cone-shaped cavity. Bricks, taken from next to the farmer's barn over the hill, and carried back one or two at a time over the course of many days, were built up into little pedestals for the candles, set at regular intervals around the periphery and roofed with tiles. Sophie was too practical to have thought of having the candles standing around unprotected.

She came back from the library while I was kicking my heels and singing quietly to myself. In one hand she had three books: a *Winnie the Pooh*, a thick hardback entitled *Introduction to Human Biology*, and a book of comic verse illustrated with colourful cartoon people. She was in a bad mood.

"It's bloody aggravating," she said, dumping down the books and struggling through the door-flap.

"What's the matter?" I said. "Look, I lit all the candles."

"It's the library that's the matter," she said. "Stupid old *cow*."

"Who?"

"That woman in charge. They only let me take out three books, and I can't ever get what I want. I have to take out two kids' books and pretend they're for me, and then ask for everything else by name and pretend that they're for my parents. It's a bind."

"Why do you have to do that?"

"Because it would look odd if I went in every week to get my parents books, and if I just picked up the ones I wanted, instead of asking for them, they think I just want to look at pictures of tits and willies. So I have to say, 'Ex*cuse* me, but my father asked if I could pick up a copy of something called—I think it was, Boyer and Davison's *Introduction to Human Biology*.' And I have to flutter my eyelids. Bloody hell."

"Can I have this one?" I said, picking up the *Winnie the Pooh*.

"Yeah. It's good, you'll like it. I'll read you some of it this evening, and the poems as well."

"We've got some *Winnie the Pooh* at school," I said. "And a picture on the wall."

Sophie had her book open, resting it on her knees. I looked over her shoulder, secretly interested by her mention of tits and willies, but the picture on the page she had opened was of a man apparently covered in pieces of meat. Disappointed, I turned back to my own book.

We read for a while and then, taking *Winnie the Pooh* with us to read before bed, set off for supper. My mother never queried our long absences from the house, as long as we were present for meals; indeed, I'm not sure that she even recognized that we were gone most of the time. She had relatively little to do with us, and Sophie always made sure that I brushed my teeth and was in bed on time. If I woke up with a nightmare, she would as often as not bring me something to drink and soothe me back to sleep. Knowing that her room was only a few yards away was a comfort that I kept myself aware of when the light was out. My mother perhaps thought that all children were as quiet and untroublesome as Sophie and I.

The story that night made me laugh with delight, and Sophie's variety of voices for the different animals had us both giggling. I went to sleep smiling, and the night was unperturbed by dreams.

• • •

He is smiling gently. "The holly bush is growing back again," he says. "I had a look. I don't think the main trunk ever died. It doesn't look the way it used to, though. One of the things that has changed."

"You can't stop things changing," I say.

"I never wanted to. Don't be stupid." He frowns. "That was what you wanted to do."

"I did?"

"All along. I never realized until—later."

"Are you sure that was how it was?"

"Yes." He pauses, looking at me curiously. "You wanted to keep everything the same. I didn't see it at the time. Strange, because you were so clever in one way, it always seemed like you were completely in control. Anything you wanted to happen, happened. You never even thought about it." He pauses again. "Maybe that's how you killed Ol' Grady. Anyway. It was like none of the ordinary rules applied to you. And when you couldn't escape them, you just broke them."

I wait for him to continue.

"I never understood what you wanted, Sophie. I never shared the way you saw things. Not really."

"Why didn't you say something?"

"I was only a kid, for God's sake! I didn't see the world the same way that you did, so I couldn't know what it was like for you."

"Is that really all?"

The same strange expression passes over his face. "I loved you. I wanted to be a part of—everything that you were. And you wouldn't let me."

I take the words and store them inside me, waiting until the time when I can see a way to use them.

• • •

My mother's pregnancy had begun to show a little by that summer: a taut-looking roundness about her abdomen. I remembered what Sophie had said, that Mummy was going to have a baby. To my eyes it looked as if her belly must be packed with something like slowly swelling frog spawn.

The days had swollen, too, becoming warm and stretching out into the evenings. It was around this time that another of the small events surrounding my childhood picture of Sophie, and her own story, took place. It started almost quietly, one morning when we had made our way down the winding road to school, and it was finished that day as well, all of it that mattered. Among the nine-year-olds were two boys who had already gained a strong notoriety for being bullies, and that morning at break there was some sort of a scuffle in the playground from which I came away bruised and crying. I can't even remember clearly what had happened; probably little more than some pushing around and name-calling. I'm equally unsure as to why they picked me; certainly not as the result of some prior, specific intent or motive. Rather, I think that it was just my turn that day to be noticed. Schoolchildren have an apparently inborn resilience to this sort of thing, apart from those who are singled out from the crowd as being more viable targets and picked on more often, and I'm sure that the incident would have been forgotten by everyone in more normal circumstances. But before the bell for end of break was rung, Sophie had seen me crying and wandered over to find out what the problem was, grinning and joking in a resigned tone with some of the girls from her year.

"What's happened to you, then?" she said, a bit more concerned now that we were out of earshot of anyone else. "Have you fallen over? Go and see Mrs. Evans."

With a measure of indignation—I fell over all the time, and didn't cry about it—I told her what had happened.

"Really?" she said, sounding less than interested. "Who was it?"

I suppose, if this had all come about a year or two later, Sophie's lack of reaction might have sparked some sense of apprehension in me. But, of course, I told her. "Been going on for a long time?" she asked, still indifferent.

"Not to me. To other people."

She patted my hand. "Don't worry about it, Mattie. Feeling better?" I sniffed and nodded. "Right, then. Off you go then." I got up and trotted away, and heard Sophie's voice as she neared the girls again, "Matthew got the shit kicked out of him by Hollis and Gregory." There was some nervous giggling. Someone said, "Got the *shit* kicked out of him, huh?" appreciatively. Another voice said, with more genuine feeling, "Those two bastards."

That morning Mrs. Jeffries asked us to put away the maths equipment we had been using, settled us down and told us a story. On the wall, the larger-than-life Winnie the Pooh and Tigger beamed down benignly. Hot sunlight had settled in patches across the room, sometimes finding a flare of colour in some plastic boxes or the fiery grain of the walnut-veneered piano. It was a Friday, and my mind drifted to thoughts of the weekend. The summer trees around the quarry had turned a deep, dark green, and the gardener sometimes set out sprinklers on the lawns, hazy and shimmering with gossamer rainbows. Lunchtime came, and lunch break, and just as we were starting to get out workbooks for the afternoon, Mrs. Colley arrived. Her face, which was normally a florid red, was paler than usual; I thought she looked slightly ill.

"Carry on with your work, children," she said, without breaking stride, and went over to Mrs. Jeffries. There was a long pause during which the two teachers carried on a hushed conversation. I bent back over my workbook, concentration broken.

"Matthew?"

My head jerked up. "Yes?"

"Could you please go with Mrs. Colley now. Leave your work where it is, you can put it away later."

Confused, and wondering what I had done wrong, I pushed in my chair and left. Mrs. Colley walked with me along the corridor to her room, which was empty. "Sit down, Matthew." I took one of the hard plastic chairs and sat. Mrs. Colley looked at me carefully. I must have seemed very nervous, because she added, "Don't be worried, dear—you're not in trouble. I just wanted to talk to you." I was not fooled: Mrs. Colley rarely talked to anyone, and certainly didn't take them to her classroom. I waited.

"Matthew, I want you to tell me what happened this morning."

I blinked. "When?"

Mrs. Colley lowered her head a little, as if making clear that the issue was serious. "At playtime. Did anything happen?"

"Oh," I said, realizing what she was talking about. Sophie must have told someone. "Nothing."

"You can tell me, dear. It's really rather important."

"Nothing," I said. "Not really."

"Hmm." She paused. "Did you cry?"

"No," I said, defensively. "Only a bit."

"Right," Mrs. Colley said, but she was talking to herself. Then to me, "Come on."

I thought we were going back to class, but instead Mrs. Colley headed towards the senior end of the building, where I hardly ever went. The corridors were deserted, with everyone in lessons, and there was the pervasive, low hum of muted conversation from many rooms. We went to the principal's office. Outside the door, Mrs. Colley hesitated, and turned to me.

"Your sister's a tough girl, Matthew." I nodded. "Well, she's hurt herself a little bit, but nothing that won't be all right in a while. OK?"

"Yes," I said. "What happened?"

Mrs. Colley tried for a smile, but the expression faltered and failed. "Come inside," she said, opening the door.

In the room were two adults—the headmaster and a woman I didn't know. Also, sitting on one of the leather chairs, was Sophie. All I noticed was an ugly-looking bruise down the side of her face. Later, I found out that she was bruised elsewhere as well, and had broken a little triangular corner from one tooth. Mr. Fergus had the same, slightly pale expression that I had seen on Mrs. Colley. He glanced at her, and she nodded.

"Hello, Matthew. This is Miss Patrick. As you can no doubt see, Sophie here's been in the wars, haven't you?" He also forced a smile. "Miss Patrick is going to drive you home now. I've already called your mother to let her know that you're going to be early."

He is talking absently, not really giving any sign that he knows I am here. I have got used to this. I sit with my wrists resting on my knees and watch him.

"You were clever. You didn't say too much—just a little, just enough, with just the right amount of hesitancy. One or two details. Where they'd touched you. What one of them had said. You must have scared the shit out of everybody in that room. Christ, Sophie, the bruises were the least of it! So, when the weekend's out, everything's back to normal. There's a couple of bullies missing from the playground, but that's about it. And the bruises fade, and it was only a milk tooth anyway. And by now all the teachers know that if Sophie Howard ever acts a little strange, well, it's perfectly understandable, poor girl." He gives a small, humourless smile. "Breaking a tooth. That's pretty thorough. You must have been proud."

I look down at my hands. The knuckles are clenched white against my knees.

# three

The summer made our garden glorious in its heat. The evenings, when Sophie and I would sometimes sit under one of the trees and tell stories, were full of the sweet, heady smell of night-scented stock, and the sky would turn a deep duck-egg turquoise as night crept in from the east. Sophie would read to me from books, or tell me old favourites from memory, or—less often, but no less enjoyably—we would just talk between the two of us. My father was still away, of course, leading whatever kind of life it was that he led between his infrequent visits to our house. I had some idea that he travelled a lot. I also realized, in a rare moment of insight, that it must have been on one of those occasional visits that the whole business with the baby had been begun. My mother, tight in her summer dresses, seemed to have settled in her drawing room like someone waiting to die. The drawing room smelled of warm wood and dusty upholstery, and although there was never any dust to be seen, the smell grew oddly stronger as the summer progressed. We avoided her there. Neither Sophie nor I cared that we had been deserted by our parents; Mummy was a shadowy figure in any case, and my father's transience was as much a part of him as Mrs. Jeffries's brightly coloured beads were a part of her. In many ways, we were unusually happy.

My father I thought I understood, to some limited degree. Mummy was an enduring paradox, walled away in her room, and even years later I never got a satisfactory picture of her; her ways were nothing like our ways, and she defied analysis, or even examination. The drawing room itself, mouldering quietly at the back of the house, was where she lived: in it, she was invisible. I preferred her that way. When she was evident in the rest of the house, her presence there was strangely irritating, and, more than that, disquieting. Everything beyond the drawing room was ours, and she had no place there. Much later, when I started trying to work out at what point Mummy had been forced back into her drawing room, I realized just how little I ever knew her. She was a complete stranger to me, utterly alien. When we wanted to spend a day out, it was always Sophie who advanced the petition—and sometimes, of course, she didn't even bother to do that. When I was with Sophie, Mummy seemed very far away.

We talked about the baby a lot. Memories of tadpoles transforming gradually into frogs linked tentatively in my mind with the pictures Sophie drew for me of sperm and ova—tadpoles and frog spawn. By now Sophie's understanding of babies and their habits was as comprehensive as she appeared to want, and her trips to the library had tapered off. I was pleased that she seemed as interested in my views as she was in demonstrating her own knowledge.

"What would you like it to be?" she asked. "A boy or a girl?"

"I don't know," I said. "A boy, I think."

"OK," Sophie said. "That would be a brother for you." But there was nothing in my mind that was prepared to make the association between the new baby and Sophie and me; nothing that understood the concept that our world was about to be expanded by the introduction of another person.

"Sophie?"

"Yeah?"

I hesitated. "What're breasts for?"

"Feeding the baby. Like on a cow," she added. "They have milk in them."

The image was striking, and vaguely repulsive. I shivered.

"You cold?"

"No." I thought for a while. "Is that all, then?"

Sophie looked at me, a little curiously. "Well, not quite. Men like them as well."

"Why? Because of the milk?"

She laughed. "No. Just because of the way they are, I suppose." I couldn't tell, from her voice, whether she was talking about the breasts or the men. She went on, "It's all really strange. And it's something that the biology books don't really talk about, either. But I think I'm beginning to understand. Parts of it, anyway." She smiled to herself.

"I think you know a lot," I said, loyally.

"Yeah."

I looked at her. She was wearing a blue and white dress and white ankle socks, her hair tied back in a ponytail. She was staring at the sky, just where it joined the treetops. The chest of the dress was braided with white.

"Sophie?"

"What?"

"Why don't you have breasts?"

"I'm too young. They come when you're older. Your body changes a lot, later on."

"Could we have a baby?"

There was a sudden glint of something in her expression,

hastily erased. "No. We're too young, Mattie. You have to be much older to have a baby. Why?"

"I don't know," I said. The conversation had moved away from its original direction, and I had forgotten rather what we had been talking about. "Will you read to me?"

A flicker of annoyance shifted her features for a second. Then she sighed. "Sure. What do you want?"

"I want . . . I want . . ." I drummed my heels happily on the turf. *"The Frog Prince."*

"Again?"

"Again," I said.

He looks at me steadily. "You *have* stayed the same, you know," he says.

"What? The same as a seven-year-old?"

"No. Of course not. I told you that some things change. But inside, that's where the real things are." He gave that small smile again. "I know you think I can't see inside you, but that's not entirely true anymore. I know you too well."

I think about that, and the more I think, the less sure I am that he is right.

He says, "Those were good times. Don't you think so?"

Carefully, I reply, "Doesn't that depend on whose viewpoint you see them from?"

He nods, pleased. "Yes. Good from yours and my point of view. Not so good, perhaps, from Hollis and Gregory's." He smiles slightly. "Or from Mummy's, come to that." It is not what I meant. He continues, "All that didn't seem so important, though. I didn't notice it, really."

"You were only a kid," I say.

"Yes."

• • •

The holly bush had thickened in the heat, so that despite the late lightness of the evenings, the leaves and Sophie's canvas lining filtered out the dying sun. I crept inside and lit the candles, striking matches from the large, stolen box that was just inside the door. Hot candle-wax and the stinging smell of freshly struck matches tingled in my nostrils. Across the floor of the holly bush were scattered books and pieces of paper, colouring crayons, some Biros belonging to Sophie, some toys of mine. I settled myself against the tree-trunk and cast about for something to do.

Sophie's books occasionally had pictures in them of naked people, but the appeal was missing somehow. Idly, I picked up one of the colourful storybooks that were stacked in an untidy pile nearby, but I had read it before, and knew the details of the pictures almost by heart. Restive, I was half ready to go and look for something else to do, when my attention was taken by a new-looking pad of paper stuck between the pages of one of the books. Smiling, I gathered together my crayon and pencils, and lifted the book and pad onto my knee. The page fell open at a strange picture, and at first I couldn't understand what was going on; the picture was of a baby, certainly, but it was twisted around and lying on its side, drawn as if it were part of something else. Gradually, I traced the shapes with my finger. Some of the words were familiar from what Sophie had told me of birth and pregnancy. The vagina would be where the baby came out. I turned the book around so that the vagina pointed downwards, as it should. Everything was wrong; the baby was upside down now. I giggled. Somebody had drawn a very bad picture of a baby inside its mother.

Interested, I turned back through the book, but there was nothing else that I could make any sense of. The words were too long and printed too small and the pictures, when there were any, seemed to be the sort of diagrams that Sophie understood but which I didn't. The funny baby had been difficult enough, but Sophie had sketched something like it for me before, so I could see the similarity.

There was a struggling, and she pushed her way through the canvas flap.

"Hi, Mattie."

"Hi," I said. "You've been a long time. I lit all the candles."

"You always do," she said, smiling. "What have you got there?" She looked over my shoulder. "Cargreaves? He's a bit boring. Can you read it?"

"Not really," I said, truthfully. "There's a picture of a baby, and it's upside down." I showed her.

"Oh, right. No, that's how it should be. He's turned upside down ready to be born. Comes out here, see? Head first."

"Really?"

"Yep. Clever, isn't it?"

" 'Spose so."

"Tomorrow's Saturday. Do you want to go to the quarry?"

I slammed the book shut with a satisfying crack. "Yeah! And look for fossils?"

"Sure, look for fossils. It's going to be really hot; I heard it on the radio. Maybe we can take a picnic lunch or something."

"Would Mummy let us?"

"Yes," said Sophie, shortly, and I knew she would be right.

"I can find lots of fossils," I said. "Last time I found millions." Sophie raised one eyebrow in disbelief. "Really, I did," I said.

"OK, maybe you did. Come on, let's see if there are any sprinklers on the lawn. I'm boiling."

My small bedroom had one window, overlooking the back garden. At night, from my bed, I could see the sky, and once, with a vivid clarity that has survived the years until now, I saw a shooting star go across one corner of the frame; a short white line that lasted in my vision for about a second. It was Sophie who told me what it had been, of course: a piece of rock, burning up high in the sky. Rather like the seabed on the hill, I found the idea of rocks burning too far-fetched to accept, and mentally fitted it into that category of information that I had long ago decided was Sophie making up stories.

Other things came in the night, though.

There was a thick, heavy pressure across my face, and my throat had shrivelled to nothing. The light that framed the doorway was broken at one side as someone started to pass, slowly, across the other side of the door. My eyes, wide and terrified, were fixed on the doorknob. My hands clutched the sheets into two hard knots. All the time, knowing what was coming, I was trying to call out for Sophie, but all that would escape from my tortured throat were pitiful gasps and wheezes. The doorknob turned, and the door opened. Just a crack. Just enough to let it shuffle in.

My body was crouched back against the headboard of the bed, the wood grating against my spine. The thing mumbled to itself as it crept along the wall, its blank face and long, trailing arms catching the moonlight eerily. It squeaked and rustled in its movements. I tried desperately to scream aloud, but nothing would come.

As Ol' Grady neared the bed, the mumblings slowly became audible, comprehensible words, repeated over and over again in a whispered chant. *You've been a bad boy, Matthew. You've been a bad boy.* The arms were moving—

And I lurched awake, my head pounding. Some sort of noise broke through from my lungs, and after that cry my chest and throat relaxed a little. I drew a shuddering breath, and tried to reach for the bedside light, but my hands were clamped down on the sheets and I couldn't make them let go. The bedroom door opened unexpectedly, and I cried out in fear.

"Shh," said a voice. "Mattie, are you OK?"

I burst into tears.

Sophie held me, sobbing, until I had calmed enough to listen to her. My breathing was coming in spurts and rushes, so as soon as I was able, she made me use the inhaler that was on the table. My hands were useless; she held it for me. She stroked the hair back out of my face and looked me over critically.

"You're an awful mess," she said. "You didn't wet the bed, did you?"

"I don't think so," I said.

"Here." She proffered a hankie. "Blow." I did so. "Wipe. That's better. Do you want something to drink?"

I stopped sniffing. "Orange squash?"

"You've done your teeth—" she began, but, on seeing my face, stopped. "OK," she said, with unusual gentleness. "Wait here. I'll leave the door open."

"And the light on," I said.

"And the light on. I won't be long."

After an age, she returned with a glass of squash. "I put ice cubes in it," she said.

"Thank you." I nursed the glass tenderly, sipping at the deliciously cool drink, making it last. Sophie usually gave me water at night, if I woke up.

"How do you feel?"

"A bit better now."

"Bad dream?"

"Yeah." My left hand clenched, and then straightened as I noticed it. I felt strangely guilty, as if my body was rebelling.

"What was it?"

"It was coming to get me," I said, and once the words were out, they turned into a torrent. "It came round the door and came towards the bed, and it was coming to get me with its arms, along the wall—"

"*What?*"

The tone of her voice made me stop instantly. I looked at her in confusion.

"What did you just say?"

"It was coming to get me . . ."

"No. After that. You said it was coming along the *walls?*"

"Yeah," I said. My voice felt uncomfortable, and small. "It always comes along the walls."

Sophie looked at me. Her eyes drilled into mine, and I could feel her weighing the words as if trying to make a decision. The expression on her face was one I had hardly ever seen—almost anger. But Sophie never looked angry. I didn't know what I'd done wrong.

It was as if she'd read my mind. "Don't worry, Mattie," she said, and held me closer to her. "You haven't done anything . . . it's not your fault. . . ." Her voice faded, and she stared for a long time at nothing. Then, "Mattie, I want you to think very hard, all right?"

I nodded.

"This—the thing you saw, in your dream. Have you seen it before?"

"Yes," I said. "Lots of times. That's the bad dream I have."

Breath hissed out of her. "OK. I didn't know that. You never told me."

"I was scared. If you think about them, they come back."

"Never mind now. Mattie, I want you to think carefully before you answer this. Think very carefully. Have you ever seen—the thing, in the dream, anywhere else? Anywhere except in a dream?"

I tried to remember. "No. No, I don't think so. It's just a dream."

"OK. Good, OK. So where the hell did it come from?"

The question didn't seem directed at me, but I answered anyway. "I don't know. But it hasn't got a face."

"Does—it have a name?"

I nodded. "It's called Ol' Grady. Can I have some more squash?"

Sophie looked right past me. "As much as you like, Mattie," she said. "I'll go and get some now. You feeling all right?"

"Yeah, I think so."

"I can't believe this," Sophie murmured, and again I felt that I was only overhearing her words, that I was not expected to comment. I kept quiet. After a long time, she seemed to focus on the bedroom again. "Was that more squash you wanted?"

"Please," I said.

"Right. We'll straighten your bed out when I get back. Shit, it's an awful mess, Mattie. You'd better sleep in my room tonight."

"Can I?" I was immediately elated, and the nightmare slipped away at last.

"Yeah. It won't hurt, this once. Now hang on while I get you another drink. And use your 'haler again."

"OK," I agreed solemnly.

As she left, I heard her say something under her breath. She had her back turned, but I caught the words. "Not Ol' Grady, Mattie. Its name was Ol' *Greedy*." And then she was gone.

That night, I curled up in Sophie's bed, warm against her back, and we slept soundly together. There were no more nightmares for a long while after.

"Ol' Grady had been dead for two or three years, by then," he says. "I only had him as dreams. When I thought about it, much later, I realized."

"What?"

"That he must have come to you as well. For longer, because you were older. I always used to wake up before he reached me." His eyes are sharp. "You must remember him, Sophie; properly, I mean, not just as nightmares. What happened? What used to happen after he reached out? What did he do?"

I stare at him in silence, not knowing what to say, how to deal with this. I notice with sudden dismay that there is a faint sheen of perspiration on his face.

"I used to try and imagine," he says, slowly. "And as I got older, the things I imagined became—more awful. They say that childhood fears are by far the worst, but that's not the whole story at all. It's when your childhood fears start growing faces that you are really afraid." He hesitates. "When I realized what you must have been through, I couldn't really believe it."

"What did you think?"

"You never really talked about him. Not properly. I know you did, a bit, when you showed me—what was left. But that's different. You didn't talk about *you*."

I swallow, with difficulty. "Do you think maybe that's the problem?"

He blinks. "Do you remember going to the quarry?" he asks. His voice has altered almost imperceptibly. "Summer was really starting to happen by then."

The candle flame splutters for a moment before recovering itself. The wind hammers on the boards and tiles of the house, and the upstairs corridors echo its sounds back.

The sun was brilliant as we walked up the hill to the quarry, and the morning was already thrumming with a vibrant warmth. The edges of the quarry were almost completely hidden by the uprushing growth of tall weeds, pink and purple with flowers, that waved lazily in the gentle breeze. My sturdy legs carried me with more confidence than I could remember them having done before, and by the time we reached the top of the hill, I was proudly controlling my breathing. Sophie was a step or so behind, smiling and carrying the picnic in a large plastic bag.

"We're at the top!" I said happily.

"OK. Let's see if there's any way at all through these things. Be careful, Mattie. Stamp them down a little and mind out for the edge." I nodded. Feeling like an explorer in a jungle, I beat down the weeds with a stick, trampling them underfoot with glee. After five minutes or so of this, we had cleared a path through to the way down. The stark expanse of the quarry stretched out below us, looking more white than grey in the direct sunlight. Only at one end, where the cages were, was the rock dark, caught in the shadow cast by that high side and lip. I swallowed. Strangely, the cages looked even more ominous now that this contrast was apparent. Almost as if they were staining the quarry themselves.

Once on the quarry floor, we cleared an area of the larger stones and settled down in it. I found a suitable anvil among the rocks to one side, and Sophie helped me to carry it to our central camp. Here also we set out the various constituents of the picnic, on carefully chosen stones. Sophie and I took turns determining the placement of the foil-wrapped packages she had prepared that morning. There were big white labels on some of them.

"You can read these," Sophie said, grinning. "They say what's inside."

"OK," I said, although a part of me was rather bored by the idea. I turned my attention to the first one, and, having read it, read it a second time. I broke into helpless laughter, rocking backwards and forwards. "It says—it says—"

"What does it say?" There was a gleam of amusement in her eyes.

"It says *dog shit*!" I burst out at last, laughter squeezing tears out of my eyes. "You wrote *dog shit* on this one!"

"Open it and see," Sophie said, solemnly. Eagerly, I tore the foil wrapping open. Inside were several sticky, shrivelled-looking brown things. I dissolved into giggles again. Finally, able to talk only with considerable effort, and still gasping a bit, I managed to say, "What *is* it?"

"You read the label; you tell me," Sophie said, but I knew her too well, and had seen the secretive laughter on her face.

"Tell me, tell me," I shouted through my giggles. "Tell me!"

"All right, calm down." She grinned. "You'll explode with giggles."

"What is it?" I peered into the package. "It *looks* like—like what you said it was."

"It's dried bananas," Sophie said, proudly. "They're really nice. You'll like them."

"Where did you get them? Bananas? Did you make it yourself?"

"You can buy them in the health food shop. They're really nice. Someone at school had them in her packed lunch."

"What's in the other parcels?"

"You can't open them until one o'clock. But you can read the labels now," she added, seeing my crestfallen look.

"Hey! Dead beetles! What's that?"

"You have to wait," she reminded me. While I read the rest of the lunch labels, laughing uproariously at some of them, Sophie went off to collect the quarry books. Seizing upon the hammer once she had returned with the bag, I quickly left Sophie to her pointless scribblings, and set about happily breaking up the more interesting-looking rocks that were scattered around. Within a few minutes I had found several of the common thumbnail-shaped shells, and was thoroughly immersed in my own world. The sun moved higher above where, strangely out of place, two small children were playing quietly.

We ate the wonderful picnic lunch, threw stones to try and knock over one of the cans, lay in the sun and made stories for each other. I listened, enthralled, to Sophie's, and she endured my rambling efforts with kindness and patience. Her scribblings went on for pages. I ran around the perimeter of the quarry, pleased at my effort, the pleasure banishing any tightness at my chest. Half an hour after lunch, with its cans of drink, I peed against the quarry wall, making patterns where the glittering stream of urine turned the hot rock dark.

When the evening drew on, the lowering sun turned a marvellous deep red. It spilled into the mouths of the cages, lighting them up like a row of blazing eyes, darkly hooded. Drawn by a half-sickening curiosity, I edged around so that eventually I was staring right into one of them. It felt like gazing into the open throat of something. The old beer cans and bits of rock on the cage floor cast short, black shadows down the depth of the opening. The bars across its mouth cut across the litter and rock, joining the dark shadows at the back. I could not see any end to the cage at all. Behind me, Sophie was gathering things together ready for our departure. With my heart beating fast, I picked up a stone and hurled it into the cage, turning and running even as I did so. There was a faint noise as it struck something metallic. I ran down and out across the quarry until I was safely away, then turned and looked.

In the cage, nothing stirred. There was no sound, no echo. It was as if the stone had been swallowed.

"You're getting really brown," Sophie said, eyeing me.

"Am I?"

# four

He has turned away from me, rested his elbows on the window-sill. The dark pane reflects his face, distorting it slightly where the old glass has rippled; when lightning scores the sky outside, the contours of his brow and cheeks are thrown momentarily into sharp relief. He hasn't spoken now for several minutes, seems instead to be searching for something beyond the cracked boards. One foot stirs uneasily on the dusty kitchen floor.

I take the time to examine things again, to remind myself of what is happening. I have a faint, unpleasant sensation that I am missing something important, but I am unable to pin it down. I try to ignore it, but the feeling won't go away.

The reasons behind this evening are starting to become clearer. I try to hold everything that he says in my head, to turn it around and around in my memory until it fits into the whole sequence, knowing that my only chance to affect him lies in understanding him, and understanding what he wants. Outwardly, I can do nothing; every time I try to move my hands, I am reminded of this. But I can listen, and, up to a point, I can talk to him. If I am careful. If I don't try to move too fast.

There is a part of me that looks on with derision as I tell myself this; but it is all I can do, and I have to do *something*.

I am very afraid.

There are areas—territories—that he refuses to explore. Not yet, at least. And there are things he will not hear from me. The bruise on my face is less painful now, but I find myself half willing it to keep hurting, to remind me of that. There are rules here.

If I detach myself from the immediacy of what is happening, I find myself curiously amazed—amazed that I could think that I knew someone so well, and yet know them not at all.

He rubs his face with one hand, pushing hair back away from his eyes, and turns towards me once more. He starts to sit down, then checks himself, remains standing, leaning against the wall. I remember his words: *I loved you. I wanted to be a part of everything that you were.* Is that true? If it's an excuse, what is it an excuse for? I don't believe he was lying; but then why am I sitting here?

He smiles slightly. He looks calmer.

My sixth birthday was one of the happiest of my life. The week had begun with salmon-pink clouds rimming the sky at dawn: I knew, because I had been awake as early as possible. The week of my birthday was also the week of Sophie's, and with great secrecy I had been preparing my presents and card for her. It was a ritual that went back as far as I could remember, with both Sophie and I pretending nonchalantly that nothing was out of the ordinary until the actual days arrived. This year, my card for her was an elaborate and time-consuming project, decorated with a good deal of stolen silver foil and milk-bottle tops. I worked on it in the privacy of my bedroom, early in the mornings, when Sophie and my mother were still asleep and the world was silent.

My mother celebrated our birthdays in her own way. There

was a selection of small, pretty-looking cakes after school, carried into the drawing room on a china plate. There was also lemonade, which helped to alleviate the dryness of the cakes, which it seemed to me might have been cooked with the dust from the drawing room; they had the same musty smell. There were presents, too: there was a quality about these that remained uniform throughout my childhood, and which I only later learned to recognize. They were universally expensive, yet out of date—the kind of gifts bought by grandparents with no sense of the current fashions in children's toys. There was a cupboard in the upstairs hallway where Sophie and I put our birthday presents each year.

My gift for Sophie was the best thing I could find. There had been agonies of doubt and soul-searching before I resolved to give it to her instead of keeping it for myself, for while I knew what a good present it would make, I was deeply in love with it myself. I had come across it in the quarry one afternoon, and something had made me stop before calling Sophie over to me. All that afternoon I had worried at it, gradually easing it from its firm seating in the grey stone, and when it eventually sprang loose—there was a small section missing on its other side, but nothing too serious—I had pocketed it, instead of surrendering it to the quarry bag with the other shells. It was quite different from anything I had seen before in the quarry: a round, spiralled shell as wide as my fist and perfectly made. Compared to the thumbnail shells that littered the rock, it was a work of art. Prising it out without breaking it had taken me the best part of four hours, but Sophie, making her unintelligible notes in the quarry books, or sunning herself happily under the oval sky, didn't seem to notice. I took the shell with me to school the next day, a warm, flat medallion in my shorts pocket. During games, when I was left alone in the classroom to read a book, I carefully painted the shell with white glue—the kind that dries clear and shiny. And so my gift for Sophie was complete.

Seeing her face when she opened the small, untidily wrapped parcel made all the time and effort well worth it. She gave me a huge hug. "It's fantastic," she said. "And you've made it shiny as well."

I nodded happily. "Do you like the card?"

"I love the card. I'm going to stick it on the wall in my bedroom where I can look at it. You must have been collecting those bottle tops for weeks." She held the card out at arm's length to admire it. "It's really good, Mattie," she said. "You didn't do this at school?"

"No," I said, feeling proud that I hadn't. "Mrs. Jeffries always tells us to draw our cards in crayon, and I wanted to make one that glitters."

"Well, you've certainly managed it. It really shines, doesn't it? And your writing's much better, too."

A few days later it was my turn. There were more dry cakes and lemonade, and, once these had been endured, more beautifully made, totally unsuitable presents. My mother sat in her chair, not meeting my eyes, tapping one foot slightly against the thick carpet. As soon as we were able to escape, Sophie and I retired upstairs to her bedroom to start the birthday celebrations in earnest.

Her present to me was neatly wrapped in red paper and tied with blue ribbon. Eagerly, I tore it open. Inside there was a small hardback book, a bar of white chocolate and a badge with *I am 6* on it.

"The chocolate's for now," she told me seriously. "I was going to get you the Winnie the Pooh book called *Now We Are Six*, but we can get that from the library. This is a bit different. What do you think?"

It was strange; she almost sounded anxious, as if she was afraid I wouldn't like her present. I turned it over in my hands carefully. On the front of the book, the title read *The Observer*

*Book of Fossils*—and then, in smaller writing, "In Colour." But what was most exciting of all was that, below the title, was a photograph of the shell I had given Sophie, almost exactly as it had been when I saw it poking out of the quarry wall.

"Wow!" I said.

"You like it? It's called an ammonite, that shell you found. You can find out all the names of the shells in the quarry, if you want."

"It's brilliant."

"I've written your name in it. See? At the front."

The end of term came in a flurry of rolled-up paintings and bags and boxes of books, emptied desks and lost Wellingtons. Mrs. Jeffries's cheery classroom was a chaotic jumble for two days, until it gradually resolved into an ordered sterility as more and more of the year's work was taken home to be stuck on fridge doors and bedroom walls. There was one brief eruption when it was discovered that I had written my name in ink pen on the inside of my desk lid, and another when Chloe Webster stabbed herself with a pair of scissors, but Mrs. Jeffries appeared unwilling to make too much of a fuss. The school playground was bubbling with parents after final assembly. The oldest children—those leaving—clumped into small groups, the boys shouting jokes at each other, boasting and trying to exceed one another's eloquent swearing, while the girls huddled in tearful clusters, hugging people they'd never liked and would probably see around the village the next day. Elements of carnival combined with grand farewells until the school appeared as if in the throes of an extravagant wake. Teachers, brittle smiles wedged on their faces, shunted children aside as they made for their cars.

Sophie and I slipped away discreetly in the confusion. We'd finished early, of course, and the sun was bright and thick in the air, so we walked slowly down the lane towards our house. The trees on the hill, surrounding the quarry, were a dark and cool-looking green, and the hedgerows had exploded into masses of weeds and grasses. The summer holidays stretched out in front of us like a journey, and the thought of them was sweet and happy.

We saw less and less of my mother. In the summer she retired in any case, preserved until the onset of autumn by the musty air of the drawing room, like something in formalin. But this summer it was even more noticeable. As her belly grew, the more she receded into the house, out of sight. The tightness of her dresses must have been uncomfortable. She seemed to be trying to compress the baby, squash it back into herself, reabsorb it before it became too insuperable an obstacle.

Sometimes, at night, Sophie and I would sit by the window in my bedroom and look out over the landscape, the hill, the trees against the sky. We told stories and waited for the stars and the moon to come out. The moon, Sophie told me once, was a place like the world, but without seas or rivers or trees or people, where all the ground was white and there was no air to breathe. In the stories, the moon was made of cheese. One man thought he had caught the moon in a pool, but it turned out to be only a reflection. Entranced, I would sit beside her and listen for what seemed like hours, until Sophie decided that it was bedtime. Once or twice, if she was in a good mood, we would have mid-night feasts of biscuits and orange squash by torchlight.

He says, "How are you feeling?"

The question comes as a complete surprise. He sounds sincere, even concerned. "I'm—OK," I reply. I keep my voice even.

"Good. I'm just going to—" He takes a candle from the windowsill, lights it from the flame of the stub burning in the centre of the floor, drips a little wax, and sets it in place. The light in the room is augmented, and the shadows recede, until he blows the first candle out. "I don't like to let them burn all the way down," he says, almost to himself, and then laughs a little. "It seems unlucky, somehow." I don't know what he means. His tone of voice strikes me as strange, as though the action of replacing the candle has confused him, dragged him out of the past temporarily.

"You're comfortable?" he asks.

"I'm OK," I say again. The boards over the windows clatter briefly as the storm tugs at them, and the fresh flame streams, dips and trembles.

He shakes his head, as if brushing away something clinging, and settles himself on the floor opposite me.

"I wanted so much to be like you," he says quietly. A draught from under the door catches me, and I shiver.

In the second week of the holiday, my father came home to us again. The lunch table was laid ready to receive him, and he appeared as if summoned by this ritual at about half past eleven. He was as tall and handsome and clean-smelling as ever, and just as forgettable. He brought Sophie and me small gifts, which we hastily unwrapped—late birthday presents, brought from America, where, we learned, he had been. His presence conferred upon the house a crowded feeling that was not entirely unpleasant; he must have remained in some way a recognized part of our family, even during his long absences. No one mentioned what had brought him back this time.

After a few days, though, the reason became suddenly obvious.

I was awakened sometime in the middle of the night by footsteps in the corridor outside my room. For a quick moment my heart leapt with fear, but then the hallway light clicked on. It was Sophie. There was more noise from downstairs, and the sound of a telephone ringing.

"Sophie?" I asked, still bemused with sleep. "What time is it?"

"It's OK, Mattie. It's—about two o'clock."

"What's happening?"

She came over and sat on the side of my bed. "Mummy's going away for a while, that's all," she said. "They're getting her clothes packed and so on."

"Why?"

Sophie frowned. "I don't know. I think maybe—"

"Maybe what?"

"Maybe the baby's ready. But I don't know," she added quickly. "It might not be time yet. Anyway, it's nothing to worry about. All right?"

"All right," I murmured, sleepily. "Will you call me if the baby's born?"

She smiled. "Sure," she said. "Sleep well, Mattie." She smoothed my pillow for me and straightened the covers. "We'll talk about it all in the morning."

I nodded contentedly, and before I knew it, I was asleep again.

The morning brought further surprises, however. I had actually made my way down to the kitchen and got the milk from the fridge for my cereal before I began to remember what had happened the night before; and then I couldn't be sure whether it had been a dream or not. Confused, I ran upstairs to where Sophie was brushing her teeth in the bathroom.

"Sophie! Did Mummy have the baby?"

Sophie glanced at me, an amused expression on her face. "Oh, so you *do* remember. I saw you go shooting down to breakfast and wondered if you'd forgotten."

"Has she?" I repeated.

"I don't know. She's not here, though. Neither's Daddy."

"Where's Daddy gone?"

She rinsed her mouth out and spat. "Your turn. I think he's gone with Mummy. There's—"

"Are we all alone?" I mumbled excitedly through my toothpaste.

"If you'll shut up a minute, I'll tell you. That's what all the phoning was last night. Do you remember Caitlyn?"

"Who?"

"She's our cousin. She's come to stay with us and look after us."

I dried my hands. "Katy? What's she like?"

"You met her a couple of years ago. No? Oh well, maybe you'll know her when you see her. She's all right. But her name's Caitlyn, not Katy. Now push off and let me get dressed."

I bounded back down to breakfast full of happy anticipation, and set about finding cornflakes and sugar. If I hurried, I was usually able to put an extra, and secret, spoonful of sugar on the cornflakes that Sophie didn't see, thus avoiding lectures on fillings and cavities. There was a strange and intangible quality of difference to the house that morning. Now that my mother had gone, it was easy to believe—if you shut the drawing room door—that she had never lived here at all. In the garden beyond the kitchen window, starlings were fighting on the lawn. I was watching them when someone came into the kitchen behind me.

"Hi, Mattie." There was a young woman standing in the doorway. She looked very tired, and her hair was a mess. She was wearing a very long, dark blue dressing gown. "What on earth are you doing up this early?"

"Are you my cousin?" I asked.

"That's right. Is there any coffee in here?"

Silently, I found the coffee jar and handed it to her.

"Don't you kids get tired at all? It's only just half past seven, you know. Little brats like you need their sleep, or something."

I giggled. She had a nice voice, although it sounded funny—different. "Have you come to live with us?"

"For a bit, yeah. I've got to try and keep you lot in control until your parents get back to deal with you. Didn't you hear me last night? I had to drive over at three o'clock. I wasn't amused, I can tell you."

Sophie arrived. "I heard you," she said. "You've got a red car."

"Well spotted. Yeah, I have."

The strangeness of her voice brought to my mind someone at school. "Are you from Scotland?" I asked.

Caitlyn laughed aloud. "Hell, no. No, I come from round here like you lot. But I just spent a year in New Zealand. You know where that is? Oh well, never mind. But they talk a different way there. So when I'm in New Zealand, people say I've got a British accent, and when I'm here people reckon I sound like a New Zealander. Or an Australian, if they can't tell the difference. See?"

"Yes," I lied. "Sophie says Mummy might have had a baby. Is that true?"

"Well, I don't really know right now." Caitlyn sat down at the kitchen table. "Sophie, love, could you make some toast or something? I don't know where a thing is in this house, sorry."

"That's OK," Sophie said, but I could tell from her eyes that she didn't mean it. I blinked in surprise. I thought Caitlyn was nice.

"But she might have a baby?" I persisted.

"Oh, I think you're right there, Mattie," she said, mock seriously. "I just don't know if she's had it yet. I shouldn't imagine so, actually. It'll take a while yet. And they'll want to keep her in to look after the baby and so on. He's come a little bit earlier than everyone expected, so it was pretty panicked last night."

"Where does the baby come out?" I asked.

Caitlyn opened her mouth, and then hesitated. Sophie said, "Out of Mummy's tummy."

I realized that Caitlyn obviously counted as an adult as far as Sophie was concerned. "I know that," I said. "What I meant was, where does she go to have the baby come out? Why doesn't she stay here?"

"Oh, right," Caitlyn said. "Well, she's gone to hospital, Mattie. They've got some wonderful doctors there who'll help everything along. You don't have any doctors here, do you?" She made a show of looking under the table.

I grinned. "No!"

"There you go, then. She's just gone away for a bit so the doctors can look after her."

"Here's your toast," Sophie said. "It's a bit burnt, I think."

"Never mind." She yawned hugely. "Look, do you guys think you can look after yourselves for another hour or two, if I just go and catch some more sleep? Then we'll all get together and work out what we're going to do."

"Sure," Sophie said. "We'll go and play in the garden. Shout out the door when you want us to come in."

Caitlyn looked relieved. "That's great. You'll be OK, won't you? Don't fall into any tiger traps or anything."

"We won't!" I said.

"Then I'll see you later. Shan't be long." With her mug of coffee in one hand, our cousin padded away into the house.

Sophie turned to me. "I bet we don't see her before lunch," she said.

"Isn't she too old to be a cousin?" I asked. "Thomas Wright has a cousin who's in his class."

"It's not important how old you are," Sophie said. "It's to do with who your mother is. Mummy's sister is our aunt, and Caitlyn is her daughter."

"What?"

She sighed. "Do you want to go out and play or not?"

"Yes please!"

"Then you'll need to put some shoes on, won't you?"

"I don't *like* shoes."

Sophie was right, and we didn't see our cousin again until midday. We spent most of the morning playing by the stream. The gardener was down by his sheds, reeling up the hose pipes and doing other, more inscrutable things, but he ignored us and we ignored him. Sophie pointed out a few slim, fast-moving black fish that arrowed through the water like slender torpedoes. The leaves on the one or two apple trees made irregular patterns of morning summer sunlight on the grass, and the air was still and warm. Most of the morning, Sophie had been a little distant, as though preoccupied with her own thoughts. When we heard Caitlyn's voice calling us back to the house, Sophie said, "You go on. I'll be along in a minute. Tell her I shan't be long."

I pursed my lips. I wasn't sure, after that morning, what Sophie's opinion of Caitlyn really was. After all, I knew she had burnt the toast deliberately. But, obediently, I ran back across the lawns to the house. Around me as I ran, the garden metamorphosed from tangled chaos to tended shrubbery, like a "before" and "after" sequence on a television gardening programme. I was expecting to see Caitlyn standing at the kitchen door, but, to my surprise, she had come out onto the grass. She was now wearing shorts and a white T-shirt.

"Hi, Mattie," she said. "Where's your sister? I've got some news for the pair of you."

"She said she won't be long," I repeated carefully. "What're you doing?"

She looked at me curiously. "Enjoying the sunshine. I thought, since it's such a good day, maybe we could have lunch on the lawn. What d'you say?"

"Great!"

"Good. Except, you're going to have to find all the food and stuff, 'cos I don't know my way around your house too well. But there's some juice in the fridge and biscuits on the side, that much I *do* know."

"I like your funny voice," I said. I meant it, but Caitlyn laughed.

"I guess that's a compliment. Thanks, Mattie. I like you, too. Ah—here's your sis."

Sophie came running up the lawn. In one hand she had a bunch of wildflowers, picked—I knew the spot—near the stone wall right at the end of the garden.

"These are for you," she said, offering them to Caitlyn. I looked up quickly enough to catch a flash of genuine surprise and pleasure in her face.

"Hey, thanks, Sophie. They're beautiful, aren't they? Mattie, we'll need something to put 'em in. Is there a jam jar or a vase, or something? No, wait a minute, important things first." Sophie and I sat down. "There was a phone call from the hospital a few minutes ago," Caitlyn said. "Your mum's absolutely fine, and she's had a baby boy. That's great, isn't it?"

"Yes," Sophie said politely. Her face was neatly expressionless.

"Your dad says everything's gone really well, and she'll be OK to come home in a couple of days or so, which isn't bad."

"Great." There was a long, uncomfortable silence.

Caitlyn shrugged. "Well, I guess we'd better do something about some food. There'll be plenty of time to make a fuss about the baby when he gets here."

"I'll go and look for a vase," I said, and went inside to see what I could find. It was good that Sophie had decided to like Caitlyn.

We found an old tablecloth and spread it on the grass. "There we go," said Caitlyn. It was something she said a lot when she was pleased. We put the flowers in a jam jar in the middle of the tablecloth, and surrounded them with biscuits and sandwiches and glasses of orange juice—fresh orange juice, which I didn't like as much as squash, but which somehow seemed to suit the strangeness of what we were doing better. Excitement bubbled inside me when we sat down around the perimeter of the table-cloth to start lunch.

"What're you guys going to do with yourselves this afternoon?"

Sophie said, "I think we might go for a walk, something like that."

"Sounds good. Mind if I come, too? As long as you're not go-ing up any mountains, that is."

I giggled.

"It's OK," Sophie said, sounding puzzled. "Mummy lets us."

"Sure, I know. But I fancy a walk. It's either that or sit in the garden and sunbathe. If you tire me out, I can always try to find my own way back."

"OK, then," Sophie said. I could understand her confusion. No one ever came with us when we went out. But then, I told myself, no one ever had lunch on the grass. Perhaps Caitlyn was different.

"Are you going to eat the rest of that sandwich, Sophie? Be-cause if not, there are some birds over there that look like they'd like it."

"They're starlings," I said.

"Is that so? You're pretty clever. You'll probably both be able to tell me lots of things."

"I've got a book on fossils," I said. "Sophie gave it to me."

After lunch, Caitlyn sent us upstairs for half an hour while she got ready. I was wandering down to see how much longer we had to wait when I heard her talking. I stopped on the stairs and listened, intrigued.

"Yeah," she was saying. "In the middle of the night. So I didn't call you or I would have woken you up." She was on the phone to someone. There was a long pause. "Yeah? That would be brilliant. We could all go out for the day. Yes, the kids, too. Of course we have to, stupid. That's what I'm supposed to be here for." There was another pause, and then she laughed. "Is *that* what's bothering you? Well, I'm sure they're both in bed by nine or so, and little kids sleep well. I know I did." I scratched my ankle.

"Yeah, I know. It's not too bad, though. Not really premature, just a bit early. Or so I'm told. You realize I haven't even set foot in this house for more than two years? I know. She's a terror." I could hear Caitlyn put her feet up on a chair as she talked. "I don't know how Mum ever put up with her, I really don't. . . . Their dad's not even home, he's at some hotel near the hospital. You'd think he'd have thought—Oh, they're fine. Mattie's a lovely little kid. He's the small one, he's six. Sophie's eight. She's pretty sweet, too. I get the feeling that she really has to look after him. Yeah. This afternoon? Well, we're all setting off into the countryside. No, we're not going far. Shut *up*!" She was laughing again. "We're just going for a walk, that's all, not a bloody arctic expedition. No I don't. I do *not*. You're awful, stop it. Yeah . . . yeah, me too. I love you, too. OK, I'll see you then, right? OK, then. Love you. Bye."

There was a clatter as she replaced the receiver and swung her feet off the chair.

"Mattie! Sophie! Come on then. Let's go and see if the natives are friendly."

Casually, I say, "You liked her."

"She was confusing. I wanted her to stay. Yes, I liked her." He sounds troubled, almost angry. Abruptly, he reaches out to the spent stub of the first candle and breaks it away from the floor, where its own wax has sealed it. He tosses the misshapen chunk from hand to hand for a while, and then flicks it away into the shadows. I hear it roll a little way, but I keep my eyes fixed on his face.

He goes on. "If we'd had a mother like—like her, then probably everything would have been different."

"Are you so sure?"

"I said probably."

"How much do you blame her?"

"Mummy? I don't know. Maybe she started it. I think she must have. Maybe she didn't make any difference at all. She certainly wasn't making any difference after a while."

"I didn't mean her. I meant Caitlyn."

His eyes widen. He starts to say something, and then cuts himself short. When he does speak, the anger is harsh in his voice.

"Don't play games, Sophie. We're through with that, remember? I'm past all of that."

"OK," I say. "Sorry."

"Don't forget. Caitlyn has nothing to do with anything. She just wandered in and wandered out again. What should I blame her for?"

I decide to say it. "For offering a choice."

He stops dead. For a second, I am terrified; but then his face relaxes slightly, and I know the chance was worth taking. He leans back a little, and I see that he is nodding almost imperceptibly.

"That's very good," he says, and there is for a second time a strange admiration in his expression. I look down, trying to keep the relief and the triumph out of my face.

# five

Sophie led the way, and for a while I thought we were heading for the quarry. She took the narrow path that cut up the hill beside the dry-stone wall, but instead of continuing to the trees at the top, she took us through a place where the wall had crumbled and cut diagonally across the field. It was the same direction we had taken when, long ago, we had been to steal bricks for the holly bush. Caitlyn kept up with us easily, and I quickly decided that she had been joking about us tiring her out; she looked as if she could keep walking all day.

"Do you guys come up here a lot, then?" she asked.

"Sometimes," Sophie said. "There's not much else to do. We play in the garden."

"Oh yeah? What sort of stuff?"

"Lots of things," Sophie said, vaguely. "Over there you can see our school."

"What, the little red building? I see it. Looks nice."

"Are you at school?" I asked. Caitlyn threw her head back and laughed loudly.

"No way! I got too big and they wouldn't let me back. Seriously, though, I've finished school now."

"How old are you?"

"Don't you know that you shouldn't ask a lady her age, Matthew Howard?" She winked at me. "Guess."

"Umm . . . I don't know."

"Go on—guess."

We were walking towards the opposite corner of the field, where there was a small spinney. A few hundred yards farther on was a larger wood, fenced off like the quarry.

"Umm . . . forty?" I hazarded.

"You are a *brat*, Mattie!" Caitlyn shouted. Sophie giggled. "I'm not that old. I'm twenty-three, that's all, and I look a good deal younger than that, I'll have you know. You're making me out to be an old woman!"

"Twenty-three's still old," I said. "I'm six."

"I knew that." She pointed ahead. "That where we're going, trail-master?"

Sophie nodded. "It's a nice place," she said. "There's a big tree that has fallen down, and it's all covered with moss. And from the edge of the trees you can look down on the village."

"Reckon we could see our house from there?"

"No. It's hidden by the hill. See?"

Sophie and Caitlyn peered back the way we'd come. Our cousin said, "Yeah, I see. Shame. You're pretty good with all this woodland lore and stuff, aren't you? You in the Guides or something? No, wait; it would be Brownies, probably."

"Some of my friends are," Sophie said.

"Well, then! Why not you, too? You get to meet lots of kids that way. And sleep in very smelly tents, of course."

"I don't think I'd like it," Sophie said, and her voice sounded smaller than I was used to hearing it, as if she was uncertain about something. Then, with more of her usual confidence, she added, "Look! We're nearly there."

"She's right again, Mattie. What's it like having a sister who's always right? Must be pretty interesting. Don't worry, Sophie, I'm just joking. Now, you want to go and sit on this tree or what?"

When I awoke the next day, there was a delicious feeling of excitement in the air. The sun was shining brightly, and the small breeze brought with it the smells of cornfields and running water. Once again, we didn't see Caitlyn until about eleven, which gave us more than enough time to walk into the village with the money and shopping list she had left us to get things for the day's meals. Quickly, with a practised eye, Sophie picked out a loaf of bread, some cheese, a bottle of orange juice, some of Caitlyn's preferred brand of coffee. I carried the wire basket for her until it was piled high with different foodstuffs. Caitlyn had given us a little too much money, and at the bottom of the list was the instruction—*Commission: spend the rest on whatever you like.*

"Does she mean it?" I asked.

"I think so," said Sophie. "What do you want?"

I looked around the mini-market. "Nothing from here."

"Then we'll go somewhere else. Do you want to carry the bag?"

"Yes."

We bought a colouring book of folk songs and fairy tales and some pencils from the newsagent's on the corner; Sophie pocketed her share of the money carefully. As we walked back, Sophie told me the stories behind the pictures in the book. One was a song, the "Raggle Taggle Gypsies," and Sophie sang it to me, to a haunting tune. The story in the song was very sad, and the music was very beautiful.

We didn't hurry home, and by the time we arrived, Caitlyn had obviously been up: there was an empty mug on the counter next to the sink, and a plate with the crusts of two pieces of toast. From the bathroom came the sound of running water.

"We're home!" I shouted. The water stopped, and our cousin appeared at the top of the stairs.

"Hi, noisy," she said. "Where's your sis?"

"She's in the kitchen. What are we doing today?"

"Wait and you'll find out," Caitlyn replied, coming down to join us. "Decent coffee! Excellent. And what's this, then? Colouring pencils? Hey! I haven't seen this sort of thing for years. Are you going to let me have a go in it?"

"If you want," I said, shyly.

"Great. Hi, Sophie. That's a pretty dress." Sophie opened her mouth, as if to say something, and then shut it again. She looked surprised. Caitlyn went on, "Today we're going to do something a little different. What time is it?"

"It's just past eleven."

"That's about right. Early, isn't it?" We giggled. "Well, I was thinking maybe we should get away from the old house for a bit, so I've arranged a little outing. And you're going to meet my boyfriend. He's called Nick and he's really smashing, so you better be nice to him or I'll cut your ears off, OK?"

We nodded solemnly.

"That's understood then. Actually, he's going to drive us so that we three can keep up with the chatter and not have to concentrate. You know the rules for boyfriends and girlfriends and that sort of thing?"

"Tell us!" I said.

"Right. Rule number one is, they're really soppy—you knew that, right? But you have to put up with it, so if there's any kissing and cuddling there'd better not be any sniggers. Got that?"

"Yes," we chorused. I grinned at Sophie.

"Second rule is, you have to make out like I did all the shopping and how I'm really amazing and I really looked after you well. Got that one, too?"

"Yes!"

"Yeah, well, that's about it, really."

"Are we going in your red car?" I asked. I had seen it parked in the driveway when we set off for the shops that morning, and had liked the look of it.

"Actually, Nick's got his own car. Why? Did you want to go in that one?"

"What colour is the other car?" I asked, doubtfully.

"Oh, I get it. It's dark green. No? Oh. We'll have to ask him if he minds driving the red one instead, then."

"You are *silly* sometimes, Mattie," Sophie said affectionately.

It was about ten minutes later that the dark green car crunched up the gravel at the front of the house. Sophie took me upstairs to put the colouring pencils away; Caitlyn and I had been playing with them, and had filled in one corner of one of the pictures in the book. "Give them a few minutes to do all the soppy stuff," Sophie said.

Nick turned out to be a very friendly-looking man, with a nice smile. I thought he and Caitlyn seemed suited to each other.

"Hello," he said. "I've been told we have to use the red car today. You must be Mattie, right?"

"Hello," I said.

"And this is Sophie. Hi there."

"Hi," Sophie said. I could tell that she was trying to accommodate this new person in the same way she had had to with Caitlyn. The struggle probably wasn't obvious to anyone except me, but I could see it clearly. "Pleased to meet you."

Caitlyn appeared from the kitchen, carrying two large bags. "Lunch and stuff," she announced.

"Caitlyn did all the shopping," Sophie said. "She's really clever."

"You don't fool me," Nick said as he took the bags and turned to the front door. "She gets everyone to say that for her."

"Do you remember showing her the fallen tree?" He doesn't wait for an answer. "I decided that was strange, when I thought about it. Unlike you, somehow."

"Things were different for a time, weren't they?"

He nods slowly. "Yeah. Sometimes—afterwards—I almost convinced myself that none of it really happened. That it was like a dream."

"Would you have liked things to stay that way?"

"I thought about that, too. I don't know. We would have been different people."

"Might that not have been a good thing?" I glance down at my wrists, and he notices.

"I still don't know. It seems too simple a solution, really." He takes a breath. "I don't want to talk about it."

"OK," I say.

In the silence, I find again that something is troubling me; not obviously, like the situation I am in, but something peripheral to it, which I should be noticing. The events of the last six hours or so have the blurry focus and poor detail of memories acquired during shock, but it is not there that I feel I should be looking. There are answers here, if I could see the questions properly. It is a tantalizing, infuriating feeling, and I am afraid that it will distract me. I shake my head a little, to clear it, and the motion jars the bruise on my cheek and makes it sting. The bruise, I have decided, is a good tool right now.

Matthew shifts position on the floor. "I almost wish she'd never come," he says.

"You'd have preferred it if there hadn't been a choice?"

He shakes his head. "There never was. We were kids, Sophie.

We didn't *have* a choice in what happened to us. I would have preferred not knowing, though."

I understand what he is saying perfectly.

Nick and Caitlyn took us along the main road away from the town. We drove for nearly an hour, until we had reached the place Caitlyn had in mind. Once the car was parked by the side of the road, we walked off at a tangent for ten minutes until we came to a broad, gravel-bedded stream, its clear water running quickly between banks edged with tufted grass. Here we settled ourselves. The bottles of squash and lemonade were placed in the stream to get cold, while Sophie and I ran about in the undergrowth. There were butterflies everywhere, and when the sun became too hot, you could quench the heat of your arms or legs in the water. The occasional drone of a car passing was a long way off, and only served to enhance the isolation of the place.

We ate a ploughman's lunch, with bread, cheese and pickles, drank the blissfully cool lemonade and lazed in the sun. After a while we started swapping stories, and gradually Sophie lost some of the slightly apprehensive shyness that had been dogging her over the past two days. When she eventually joined in, even the two grown-ups were impressed. We had been telling fairy tales to begin with, but Sophie changed the subject to ancient myths and I listened, enraptured, to stories of heroes and gods and creatures from the underworld. Somehow, we then ended up telling jokes, and after that everyone except me had a little lie down in the sun. I set off to walk along the bank of the stream and see how far I could get in half an hour. I had Sophie's wristwatch with me to check the time by.

When I rejoined the group, the picnic had been packed up again, and the other three were laughing at some joke or story that I had missed. We walked back to the car with the afternoon sunlight becoming more orange. My pockets were full of pebbles and my head full of questions and ideas.

The phone was ringing when we opened the front door. Caitlyn rushed to pick it up.

"Yes? Speaking. Yes, that's right. How is she?"

I put the stones in my room and helped put the remnants of the food into the fridge. Sophie helped; Nick had joined Caitlyn and was listening in on her conversation.

I heard the receiver click into place. The two grown-ups came through to the kitchen.

"That was your dad," Caitlyn said, brightly. "Seems your mummy's done really well. She's coming home tomorrow."

Sophie's eyes widened, and then her face went blank, as if someone had shut it off.

"Will Mummy bring the baby?" I asked.

"That's right, Mattie."

"What's the baby called?"

Caitlyn shrugged. "I don't know. I expect you'll find out sooner or later."

Nick said, "How is she?"

"Fine, by all accounts. Must have a constitution like a mule," muttered Caitlyn, audibly. In a normal voice, she continued, "You'll be able to see your brother soon. That's going to be good news, isn't it?"

"Yes," I said. "Will you still be here?"

Caitlyn hesitated. "Ah—well, Mattie, no, I won't. Not for much longer, anyway. But we've got lots of time before that, so we'll make the most of it. And when Mummy comes back, I want you and Sophie to be really understanding and helpful, 'cos I imagine she'll be pretty tired. You know, make her breakfast in bed and get her lots of tea and all that."

"Yes," I said, even more doubtfully.

For a moment Caitlyn seemed at a loss. Then, with a big grin, she said, "Come on, then. Let's play I spy. Do you want to stay in here or go outside?"

That night, I lay awake looking at the summer sky outside my window, thinking how nice everything was. I thought back on the wonderful afternoon by the stream, and the red car, and the colouring pencils. As I turned over and closed my eyes, I remembered something else also. I had gone back downstairs to retrieve my colouring book and pencils from the hall, where I had left them. The door to the spare bedroom was standing open, and I could hear Caitlyn talking inside.

"Do you think I've had too much sun? I spent a long time outside yesterday, too. Better be careful, or I'll end up like a peeled prawn."

Nick said, "You'll be OK. Are you going to have a shower?"

"That I am. I've got half the heath in my shoes, I reckon. Well? What do you think?"

"About what?"

"You know. *This*. This place."

There was a long silence. "Truthfully? I don't know. It's not as bad as you make out. They seem nice enough kids."

"Yeah, I know. I'd take little Mattie home right now if they'd let me. But there's something strange about Sophie, like she knows more than she's letting on. D'you get that feeling?"

Nick considered. "No, not really. Like I said, she seems OK to me. Bright kid."

"Too right. She knows things I don't know. And her stories were pretty damn good, too. Maybe I'm just overreacting still. I haven't got over the shock of being dragged out to the recluse's abode yet. Nearly scared me shitless, middle of the night and all."

I padded upstairs with my book, smiling to myself that

Caitlyn liked me. In the corridor below, the voices continued, sometimes murmuring, sometimes laughing. And, later, in bed, I wondered what it might be like to live somewhere else, to go home with someone different and never come back.

The next day, my mother came home.

It was all over very quickly; my father drove her to the house. With them was a white plastic carry-cot with the baby wrapped up inside it, silent among blankets. For once, my mother seemed to notice Sophie and me: she took us into the kitchen, and, resting the cot on a chair, let us see the baby. Its tiny face was swollen and dark, and in front of its mouth it held two minute fists, as if in the throes of some terrible rage.

"This is your brother," my mother said. We both looked at the baby in silence, unsure of what to say. "He's asleep at the moment."

Caitlyn came through to the kitchen. "Isn't he adorable?" she said. "Look at him—all snuggled up." My mother shot her a glance.

"Have Matthew and Sophie behaved themselves?" she asked.

"Oh, they've been perfect," Caitlyn said easily. "Nick! Come and have a look at him. He's gorgeous." When I looked at her face, though, I suddenly had a strong feeling that she was concentrating more on saying the right things than being genuine.

"Hello," Nick said to my mother, awkwardly. My father was somewhere in the background, moving between rooms, sorting things out.

"What's the baby called?" I asked.

"Have you decided yet?" Caitlyn added.

My mother nodded. She didn't look tired, as Caitlyn had said she might; she looked the same way that she usually did. "We've decided on David," she said.

"That's a nice name," Caitlyn said. "Hi, Davey." The baby stirred uncomfortably, and made a little coughing cry.

"Really, we mustn't keep you," my mother said. "I'm sorry to have troubled you like this, really I am." She pressed a sealed envelope into Caitlyn's hand. "I'd be most grateful if—"

"Oh, come on," Caitlyn said. "Families don't do that sort of thing. Besides, I really enjoyed myself. It was great fun, wasn't it? We did lots of things, and these two were good as gold. In fact, it's a shame I don't see more of them. Perhaps they could come round once in a while? It'd be no problem, I promise."

"That's very kind," my mother said, and I saw Sophie's face—which had become tinged with expectation—fall at the words.

"It would be lovely," said Caitlyn, but now that I had noticed Sophie's reaction, I thought I could hear defeat in her voice as well. She put the envelope on the table and left it there.

"I guess we'd better be off," she said to Nick. Then, abruptly, she bent down and kissed the end of my nose. "Bye, Mattie. Keep good care of yourself, you hear? Colour some pictures for me."

"Bye, Caitlyn," I said. It was strange, I hardly felt sad at all.

She kissed Sophie, too, "Bye, Sophie. I really liked the tree you showed me. Take care, OK?"

"Bye," Sophie said, carefully. "Thank you for looking after us."

"Run along, you two," my mother said. As we left the kitchen into the garden, I could hear her talking to Caitlyn again; the mention of colouring pictures seemed to have caught my mother's attention. I could hear her saying, "At least let me reimburse you for . . ."

There was a low smear of cloud in the morning sky as I followed Sophie down the garden. I saw a bottle top lying in the grass, near where we had eaten lunch on the lawn. Sophie was walking very fast, heading for the holly bush.

"Wait for me!" I said, but she ignored me. I reached the holly bush after her, and pushed my way in through the curtain of dark leaves clumsily, ignoring the scratches I got as a result. Sophie was sitting in the middle, her back to the trunk, breathing hard as if she had been running. I knew immediately that something was wrong.

"Sophie? Are you OK?"

As I watched, her hands gripped the canvas covering the floor, then unclenched. She opened her mouth a little way, and made a noise that was almost like the beginning of a sob. As if this was all that was necessary to break open what she had been holding back inside, she struck the ground with both hands, and cried out loud, "You fucking *bitch*! Fucking bloody cocksucking *bitch*." There were tears running down her cheeks, but instead of crying she shouted obscenities, on and on, words I had never heard and didn't understand. I sat in terrified silence until, at last, her voice grew quieter, and finally she stopped. She was still breathing in little irregular gasps, but her face had become more normal again.

She seemed to notice me for the first time. The last of the anger and violence went out of her, and she reached across and hugged me to her tightly. With my face pressed into the comforting warmth of her shoulder, she whispered, "It'll be OK, Mattie, it's going to be all right. Don't worry, everything's going to be OK." I hugged her back, scared for her, not knowing what was happening, not aware that there *was* anything wrong, anything I should have been worried about. After a long time, she pulled away a little and looked into my face.

"Hey," she said, and there was a fleeting glimpse of one of her old smiles. "Don't look frightened. Everything's going to be all right. I promise. You'll be all right. I'll look after you. You know that, don't you?"

"Yeah," I whispered.

I was only six; I really thought she was talking to me.

# six

We stare at each other across the boards. The hollows of his eyes are pooled in shadow, and the candle on the floor makes an eerie reversal of the normal contours of his face. It makes it difficult to judge what he is thinking. I am starting to realize that the need to make that sort of judgement about him has become very strong.

Matthew frightens me: I have never seen him like this, never suspected, before tonight, that he was capable of anything of this nature. I have been taken by surprise, and now there is nobody except myself to look to. The pieces of Matthew's story are joining together, beginning to form a more coherent whole than before. Disjointed memories are giving way to a more consistent, more linear account. I do not know, yet, where this is leading, but I am sure that what happens here, now, in this room, will be determined by what happened years ago.

The dream-like quality of our conversation is offset sharply by the constant reminders of the world outside—the storm, the sounds of the wind and rain, the sudden whipping to and fro of the candle flame. Once there has been a crash as a slate has torn from the roof and shattered against something hard; at other times, there have been void-like moments of quiet when the wind has dropped, and only the hammering of the rain has continued in the background. I can't remember a night as fierce as this.

I have tried to stop myself regretting how I came to be here; there is no point, and I need my concentration on what is happening *now*, not what happened hours ago. But every so often, I can't help but think—there must have been a way to avoid this earlier! Before it reached this! I don't think there was, though. Matthew has kept his secrets too well, and it is only now that I am being allowed to see them, being allowed to share them.

But now I have a secret as well. Not much, yet, but the first taste of something. Because I am getting to know Matthew Howard from the inside for the first time, and although I don't yet know how to use what I am discovering, it is the only edge that I have. I don't mean to waste it. There is still enough time.

Life almost returned to the way it had been; almost, but there were subtle differences. My father was around the house more often. My mother, who had practically disappeared from our lives for the past few months, was now to be seen on her normal circuit of movement around the ground-floor rooms. Upstairs, the books and shelving were cleared out of the little room at the end of the corridor, and a crib was brought down from the attic and set up. The baby, whose normal expression of rage occasionally softened into something resembling normality, became a part of life overnight. In his white room with the pale blue blankets and curtains, we could hear his baby-noises sometimes when walking along the top corridor. Our family doctor, a large man with cool, dry hands, dropped in one morning, looked the baby over and pronounced him fit and well. Maybe, in our sleepy little village, he had nothing better to do.

A house with five people in it was unusual and claustropho-
bic. Sophie and I went to the quarry to escape.

Soon, the first of the wasps were evident in the garden, scanning the trees in the orchard and zooming around the drainpipes
of our house. Once the initial excitement over the arrival of the
baby had died away, I grew used to the idea, although it was
not nearly so much fun as I had imagined it might be. There was
no pram to push, for example, although my mother sometimes
took the carry-cot out into the sun on the edge of the lawn. That
in itself was a new departure; the back garden was usually territory into which my mother never strayed.

Being six was not noticeably different from being five; I still
played the same games, was scared of the same things, liked the
same stories. Growing older was a transparent process, and I
only saw the evidence of it later, and from a new perspective.

Sophie and I went fishing for sticklebacks in the pond behind
the hill. The sunlight was hazy through the trees, and played
across my back as I bent, laboriously tying a worm on the end of
my piece of cotton. The little fish lived in and among the old
bottles and cans and pieces of metal that had been dumped long
ago in one end of the pond. Once they'd attached themselves to
your worm, you could haul them straight up out of the water
and they wouldn't let go.

We returned home happily exhausted. My mother had prepared supper while we had been out; we ate it quietly. We had
both long since given up trying to interest her with what we
had been doing. At bedtime, Sophie told me a story about a fool
who won a princess's hand in marriage by presenting her with a
dead crow and some mud. I found the idea extremely funny, and
giggled quietly to myself once or twice as I fell asleep.

In the night, in my dreams, there was a rustling in the corridor. Only now I recognized some things that had not been there

before: the blue curtains were dark against the pale walls, and there were bars all around me. The crack of light down the hinge of the door was abruptly covered as something passed outside. The door opened, and it shuffled into the room.

My body had frozen, motionless, unable even to breathe, as the long-armed, faceless figure of Ol' Grady edged along the wall, its mumbling words taking shape in my memory. *If you're a bad boy, Matthew, Ol' Grady will come.*

And with the cry half out of my throat, I shuddered awake.

I must have made some noise. The light down the corridor snapped on as I fumbled for the inhaler that always rested on my bedside table. Sophie opened the door and slipped into the room.

"What is it?" she whispered as she knelt down beside the bed. "Is it the same one?"

I nodded helplessly, and took another gulp of spray. Gradually, the aching tension in my upper chest relaxed, and I found it easier to exhale.

"OK, it's all right now," she murmured, and brushed the hair back out of my eyes.

"Sophie, I'm scared," I whispered back. "There were bars."

"There were bars round you?" she asked, understanding immediately.

"Yes."

"Shit." She paused. "Mattie, you've got to listen to me. Ol' Greedy's gone now. He's dead. Do you understand? It was just a bad dream." She stared into my eyes, as if willing me to believe her, and saw it was no use. "Shit," she said again. There was a struggle evident on her face, as if she wasn't sure what to do. Then she came to some decision.

"Do you feel better?"

"Yes," I said. "It was just a dream, I think."

She rubbed my head and smiled. "You *know*, you mean. That's all it was, Mattie, just a bad dream. Ol' Greedy's been dead for a long time. You want to see?"

I looked at her with incomprehension.

"Put on some trousers and shoes," she said. "And your coat. It's cold outside."

"Are we going outside?" I asked. "It's the middle of the night!"

"Yeah, I know. Don't worry, I'll be with you. Just put some clothes on, OK?"

"OK," I agreed, confused but unwilling to let such an opportunity for excitement pass. I had no idea of what Sophie was thinking. She went back silently to her room and reappeared a few minutes later with clothes pulled on over her pyjamas. I was having trouble with my shoelaces, so for once, instead of letting me tie them myself, Sophie knotted them quickly and neatly.

"There. Are you ready?"

"Where are we going?" I asked, fascinated.

"I'll tell you on the way. Quiet, now. You don't want to wake the baby."

"No," I agreed.

We went downstairs, through the silent and empty kitchen. Sophie unbolted the back door, and we stepped out into the moonlit garden. Shadows under the bushes were black as oil, and the sky was riveted with stars.

"It's dark," I said.

"I've got a torch," Sophie replied. "Don't you worry. This way, now." We started down the lawn towards the stream. As we walked, Sophie talked to me quietly.

"It's not easy to understand," she said. "I want you to try, though. You see, Ol' Greedy doesn't exist. He's like a fairy story, right?"

"Right," I said, doubtfully.

"He's just an idea to frighten people with. He's—ah—like a bogeyman."

"I've got a book about a bogeyman," I whispered.

"What I'm trying to say is, even if Ol' Greedy frightened you once, he won't again. Careful, this bit's slippery."

We crossed the little bridge and made our way through the orchard. The little grouping of sheds loomed up out of the night. Sophie clicked the torch on, and the shadows leapt up like black flames. I reached out tentatively and held her hand.

She smiled. "There's nothing to be frightened of. It's a bit spooky, isn't it?"

"Yeah," I said in a small voice.

"It's OK, though. I'm here." We passed by most of the sheds and came up against one that was crouched against the wall at the end of the garden. Sophie took a key from her pocket and held it in the torch beam as she undid the padlock.

"You're not to be scared, OK?" she said. "You've got to be brave."

She opened the door to the shed. For a moment, there was nothing, and then a long arm snaked out of the opening, brushing against the door frame. My heart stopped for a long second, and then pounded in my throat. I gripped Sophie's hand as if I were drowning.

The door swung fully open. Hung on the back of the door was the skin of Ol' Grady.

Sophie played the torch on it. "You see?" she said.

I looked. It wasn't a skin; it was some sort of coat.

"Come in," she said. "I'll show you."

Still nearly rigid with fear, I followed her without protest into the shed. Sophie shut the door carefully behind us, put the torch down on a shelf, and seated herself on the edge of a big metal drum. Silently, we stared at Ol' Grady.

"What is it, then?" Sophie said, after a minute or so had passed.

I swallowed. "It's a coat," I said.

"But you thought it was something else . . . ?" she prompted.

"Mm," I said. "It looks scary."

"There's nothing scary about a coat," Sophie said. "This is a special coat. It's for rainy weather. They wear them on boats. It's called an oilskin. You can see it's quite long, yes? So your knees keep dry as well."

Reduced to these mundane descriptions, the skin of Ol' Grady did seem to lose some of its terror. I relaxed my grip of Sophie's hand just a little, but kept hold of it firmly just the same.

"It's just a coat," Sophie said. "If you put it on normally, it looks like a raincoat. It's got a hood, see?"

"Mm."

"Let go a second," she said. She took the oilskin down from its peg and held it up. "It's way too long for me," she said. "I'm going to look like a dwarf if I put this on." I giggled nervously. "Do you want to try it?"

"I don't know," I said. Gradually, the blind panic I'd felt when the arm of the coat had swung round the door was seeping away. I reached out deliberately and touched the coat. It felt heavy and smooth.

"Go on," Sophie said. "It's all right." She helped me put my arms into the sleeves, and then drew it around me. The hem of the oilskin trailed on the ground. "It's just a coat, right?"

I laughed. "Yeah, it's just a coat." The laughter welled up inside me. "It's just a *coat*!" I said. Sophie nodded, smiling.

"You want to pretend to be Ol' Greedy?" she said.

"Yeah. How?"

"Take it off." She helped me. "Now, just turn it around, see? Put it on back to front. Now you look like it's not a coat at all. And if you put the hood up now, you look like you haven't got a face. Go on, try it." Nervously, I pulled the hood up over my head. Inside, the coat smelt warm and slightly sweaty. I found there was a rip in the cloth that I could see out of.

"Wow," Sophie said. "Pretty scary, Mattie. I think you'd better make some ghost noises now."

I giggled. "Whoo!" I said quietly.

"Louder than that. No one can hear us down here."

"Whoo! Whoo!"

"That's better. You're a really scary ghost."

"I am?"

"Yeah."

I flapped my arms. "I feel scary." Sophie grinned.

"And if you walk with your back to the walls, then no one can see the opening," she went on. "Understand? So it doesn't look like a coat anymore."

"You've been a bad boy, Matthew," I said. "If you're a bad boy, Ol' Grady will come." I pulled the hood down again. "So Ol' Grady isn't real?"

"No. He's just an old coat. Pretty silly, huh?"

"Yeah," I said. "Really silly." I paused. "The bars . . ."

"The bars in the dream?"

"Yeah. Those could be bars on a cot, couldn't they? Like the baby has."

"That's right. I think that's how it was, Mattie."

"But it was all a long time ago, and now Ol' Grady's dead." I yawned. "I think I understand."

"You ready to go back to bed now?"

"OK," I said, and yawned again. "Put Ol' Grady back." We hung the oilskin on its peg and went outside. There was the first lightening of the sky beginning to show behind the hills to the east. I held the torch while Sophie locked up the shed again, and we hurried back through the cold night air to the kitchen door.

Once inside, Sophie settled me down again in my bed. "Feeling better?"

"Yeah," I said.

"OK. You're a pretty brave boy, aren't you?" I blushed.

She closed the door quietly behind her, and I heard her footsteps move down the hall, and then the gentle click of her door closing.

He moves his hands against each other uncomfortably; his voice has become tense. I sit frozen against the wall, not moving, not speaking, trying to give away nothing of what I am thinking.

He says, "You can only have been about five. What did you do, Sophie? How did you kill Ol' Grady?" He lapses into silence briefly. Then, "She always seemed afraid, almost. Afraid of you. Half hating you, but too afraid to do anything." There is a rough edge to his laughter. "Which one of you ended up the victim? Can you tell me that? It was you to begin with, but you sorted that out pretty fucking quickly. Things got turned around. By the time you'd finished, Ol' Grady was dead, and Mummy was just a shell. Venomous, yes, but nothing compared to what she must have been before. When you knew her."

"I don't know what you mean." But, if I am truthful, I begin to think I do.

"You killed Ol' Grady, and you forced her back into her dusty drawing room, but you were too late to stop the dreams. There wasn't anything you could do about that. The memories were still there, somewhere, but they weren't real; they couldn't be dealt with in the same way. You must have felt—angry, about it. Like you'd failed. You didn't like to fail at things."

"Lose control, you mean?"

"Exactly." I smile to myself, slightly. He says, "It must have hurt you. I understand. I know how you felt."

I blink at that. How much did Matthew understand? How much did he know, back then? It is a frightening thought; to hear him speak, you could imagine him completely innocent of the realities around him, oblivious for ages to the truth of what—who—Ol' Grady was. Is that how it was? Or is it just how he wishes it was? I hear only what he says. And this, this last, seems almost a confession.

After a while, he continues. "I went back to the quarry, you know." It seems a statement made at random, and I wait for him to follow it up, but he doesn't. Instead, he gets to his feet, paces the length of the kitchen, peers between the cracks of the plywood sheets that cover the window. There is less lightning now, and his face remains dark. He seems to be looking for something, and it occurs to me abruptly that he is trying to see the hilltop behind the house where the quarry lies. The hiss and beat of rain echoes upstairs, and there are the creaks and mutterings of the old house around me. For a minute, while he stands there motionless, it is almost as if I am alone. I feel a sharp, overpowering urge to start crying, to bury my face in my arm and forget where I am. It would be very easy.

I say, "What can you see?"

He looks round, surprised by my voice. "Not much. The rain's too thick. . . ." His voice trails off absently, and he turns back to the window. He is there for a while longer, and then he goes back to his place opposite me. The candle casts his shadow large and fluttering on the plaster of the wall, and in that instant

I can imagine Ol' Grady sliding around the walls of the nursery, reaching for him through the bars.

The summer was nearly over. Sometimes the smell of bonfire smoke from the farm reached us on the breeze.

It happened in the night, and Sophie shook me awake to the sound of vehicles pulling up on the drive outside. There were voices downstairs. There was an ambulance, and Doctor Roberts was there, too. In the kitchen, with Sophie and me standing by silently, he told my mother about cot deaths, how it could happen at any time, for no reason. There was nothing she could have done. My father was not home. My mother sat like a statue, her hands folded precisely as alabaster on the smooth surface of the table.

Afterwards, I asked Sophie, "Is the baby dead, then?"

"Yeah," she said.

"Oh," I said. We sat on the stairs. There were voices still in the kitchen, and then a crunch on the gravel of the driveway as a car arrived.

"Is Mummy upset?"

"I don't know."

"Doctor Roberts said there wasn't anything we could do," I said.

Sophie nodded. "Yeah. I know."

A door slammed. We sat there, ignored, as the rest of the house went about their business around us.

# seven

I struggle to find something to fill the silence. In the end, I say, "What did you feel? Then?"

"I hardly know anymore." His voice is hoarse, unpleasant. "A lot happened since then, wouldn't you say? It's not so easy to disregard everything else."

"Can't you—try to?"

He sighs. "I don't know what I felt. Some kind of disappointment, I suppose. Nothing much. Nobody seemed to feel anything. It wasn't just me."

"You don't think they were just keeping it hidden?"

He shakes his head. "I don't know. That sounds more . . . humane, doesn't it? Maybe that's what it was."

His eyes dart around the room, as if he is looking for something. He says, "The next time I saw Caitlyn was at Mummy's funeral. She was older. She saw me, but either she didn't recognize me or she chose not to. She was with a man I'd never seen before. I think they were married." He runs his hand irritably through his hair. "I didn't mind. She was just something else that had passed out of our lives by then. It's strange. She didn't look happy, and I was pleased."

"Would you still be, now?"

"I shouldn't think so. I was only eleven. Everything was—everything was coming apart. You know. Maybe I felt that she deserved it."

"What for?"

"Oh, shut up, for fuck's sake." He pushes his hand through his hair again, and lets his brow drop into his palm. He sits there, cradling his head, and I watch him without speaking. Again, I am afraid at what I have glimpsed.

If Matthew was predictable, everything would be fine; but he is not, and his changes of mood and of interest frighten me. I know, when I am honest with myself, that I am in more danger here than I thought at first. I also know that, realistically, I have very little chance of developing things to my advantage. I am not even sure whether what I am doing—waiting, and watching—is the wisest course, whether I shouldn't instead try to confront him again. I squeeze my right eye closed, and feel my cheek burn; no. I tried confrontation before, and it got me nowhere then.

I am beginning to feel that there is nothing I can do, that there is no way out of this. Matthew, opposite me, head down and not speaking, is simultaneously my enemy and the only hope I have. It is ridiculous. I don't even know exactly what I am trying to escape.

I have my small store of weapons: the bruise on the side of my face, the reminders of the world outside, the scraps of information about Matthew that I keep telling myself will eventually build into something I can use. What if they never do? What if there is no coherence in what he's saying? The irony is that, to avoid whatever madness this is, I am going to have to trust him, however hard that may turn out to be. I bite down on my lower lip sharply. I know I can do it, if I keep strong.

He raises his head, clasps his hands together in front of his mouth, and stares at me. I realize that I hardly know the man who is looking out of his eyes.

"What are you thinking?" he says.

"Nothing."

"Tell me."

"I really don't know. I'm too frightened to think."

He looks surprised at that. "You don't have to be frightened. But at least you're being truthful now. That's good."

I have to bite back laughter; the confession wasn't planned, only came out that way by chance. I really *am* too frightened to think. That thought sobers me, and I realize that if I keep speaking what is in my head, I will make a mistake—sooner or later. The laughter in me vanishes instantly.

Between then and my ninth birthday, there was a fallow period, where nothing of great joy or great sadness happened, and which memory has compressed into one or two sharp images. Watching rabbits at dusk in the fields across the lane. A playground scrap where, for once, I came off best. Sophie's annoyance when, nine years old, she had to wear braces on her teeth for a time to correct some small irregularity—although I remember that nobody teased her about them. Holding hands with Elizabeth Anne after school, and hoping fervently that no one had noticed. Catching a bird that had flown into the kitchen through the open door, and feeling its madly beating heart before I let it go. Good memories, all of them. And, of course, I grew taller, and older, wore long trousers to school for the first time.

All this time, though, it was still just the two of us. The summer holiday in which Sophie turned eleven, and I nine, saw us playing in the same places as three years previously, although perhaps the games were different.

Walking back from school, the air was thickly fragrant with bonfire smoke. A silver bank of cloud hung low down in the western sky, although the light was clear enough. The hedges and roadsides were laden with the browns and reds of autumn, and the conker trees were heavy with spiky fruit. Our class was doing fruits and seeds for science, so I knew several of the more common species by name, and understood how wind dispersal worked for dandelions and sycamores, but not for holly. Sophie and I were chatting away about the day's work, which teachers we liked and what had happened. We saw less of one another during the day than we had before; among the older children, the boundaries between different year groups hardened so that, even at break time, we hardly ever spoke.

"I'm building an aeroplane," I said.

"Where are you going to fly to?"

"Silly. A model. There's four of us, and we've got most of the wings done now. It's made out of balsa wood, and we're covering it with paper and dope and stuff."

"Yeah? When's it going to be finished?"

"Before half-term," I said airily. In fact, there had been arguments over who should design the camouflage, and half-term was quite an optimistic date.

"I'd like to see it when it's finished," Sophie said. She pointed up across the hill we were passing. "See there?"

"What?" I asked. It was the old farm where we had once stolen bricks.

"They're selling it," Sophie said. "Tessa's dad works there sometimes. There's a really big company that's moved in and bought them up. I don't know what they're going to do, but they're obviously after land around here."

"Do you think they'd want our house?" I asked.

"I don't know. We're quite a bit farther away, you know. And I haven't noticed anything." She meant she hadn't overheard anything. "Probably not. We're in a funny little dip, you know? Where the stream cuts down. So probably it's too awkward a site for anything serious."

"Is that why the fields are empty?"

"The ones behind the house? Yeah, that's right. But all these will be, too, soon enough." She waved a hand to indicate the farmland off to the side of the road. "Anyway, I thought it might be useful to know. So little happens around here normally." She shook her head.

"Mr. Fergus wanted to see you, didn't he?" I asked.

"Yeah."

"What about?"

She turned and grinned. "Nosy little bugger. He wanted to talk to me about schools. You know, where I'm going to go after this. It's exam time next year."

"Why didn't he talk to Mummy?"

"I think he has. They seem to reckon I could get a scholarship. It would mean extra lessons and stuff."

"And? Are you going to try?"

"I don't know. Fergus is only interested because of the prestige factor for his shitty little school. And it's not as if we *needed* a scholarship financially. You wouldn't catch Mother talking about a bursary instead, for example. So I really don't know. I don't know if I want a scholarship."

"You're going to pretend to be stupid, then?"

She laughed quietly. "That sort of thing, maybe. They think they've sorted it all out between them, I expect. I'll think about it."

We walked on in silence for a while, enjoying the waves of

light and shadow racing across the hillside. A strong wind was starting to blow; we could see its full effect in the distance, where trees were rippling on the skyline.

"I thought, once the plane's done, I could launch it from the top edge of the quarry," I said. "See if it really flies."

"Yeah, why not. But don't bring any of the others, will you? It's good to have a place that's just our own."

"I know," I said. "If it's finished in time, we could do that at half-term. If I can borrow it for a few days. And if it doesn't rain, of course," I added doubtfully.

"Unpredictable thing, the future," Sophie said. "You can never be sure what might happen. You can't even imagine it, necessarily. That's chaos theory for you."

We walked round the second slight bend in the road and our house came into view, huddled in its long garden in a dip in the land. In the drive, my father's car was clearly visible.

"What do you think Daddy's doing here?" I said.

"God knows. Another surprise visit. Maybe we'll get something decent for supper." Her tone was hard, unpleasant.

"It's not his fault," I said uncomfortably. Sophie shot a glance at me, one eyebrow raised.

"What's not?"

"Him being away all the time."

"It's not? What, you think it's his work or something that keeps him away?"

I stared back at her, not knowing what to say.

"Shit, you didn't really think that, did you?" She shook her head again. "Christ. You don't get the impression he just doesn't like being with us all that much?"

"I don't know," I said.

She sighed, and then slapped my arm gently. "Hey. Sorry. I didn't mean to snap."

"It's OK." There were birds trailing across the sky near the wood, and I followed them with my eyes until they swept out of sight.

"Hey," Sophie said after a pause, "did I tell you I got my period?"

"Did you?"

"Yeah. I'm the first in our class, I think."

"How does it feel?"

"Odd. It's nothing awful, though. I got really worried at one point, all that stuff about pains and cramps and things, but none of that's happened."

"Have you told Mummy?"

"No. Why, do you think I should? Like, walk into the drawing room and say, 'Hello, Mummy, did you know your daughter's a functioning woman now?' " She giggled. "I don't think so. I used some loo paper, and then bought some towels and things in town."

"Where did you get the money?" I asked. She looked at me strangely.

"I've been saving up," she said. "Why? You think I nicked it or something?"

"No," I said, hurriedly. "That's not what I meant."

She stared at me almost angrily for a second, and then her expression changed, and softened. "Ah, shit. Yeah, of course I nicked it. Anyway, who's going to do that sort of thing for me if I don't do it myself? One thing you do learn in this household, Mattie, is that you've got to look after yourself." We turned into the drive, and our feet scrunched on the gravel. "One other thing, though. If you need any cash for anything, don't for heaven's sake try to take it yourself. You'd balls it up. Let me know, and I'll give you some, OK?"

"OK," I said, secretly rather shocked. And then, because we were about to enter the house, I stopped. "Sophie?"

"Yeah?"

I hesitated. "What did—I mean, how did you do it? Take it from her bag?"

A slow smile spread over her face. "No, stupid," she said, and slapped me lightly again. "She'd notice. I took her cash card. The code's written down in the telephone book. Pretty stupid, 'cos there's no area code and this region uses five figure phone numbers." She shrugged. "C'mon, let's get something to eat."

What Sophie had said about my father not really liking us preyed on my mind. That night in bed, I realized that she was undoubtedly right, and was confused that I hadn't reached the same conclusions myself. Five of the children in my class had divorced or separated parents, but there was no way that I would ever have counted myself as a possible sixth. My parents weren't separated; my father simply hardly lived with us, that was all. When I began to think of the situation in these terms, I found myself scared and worried. I found it more difficult still to see that the strange relationship between my parents, no matter how tenuous, was apparently a permanent one. In the end, I took some of these fears to Sophie. We were walking by the edge of the wood, supposedly collecting seeds for a project of mine.

"They say a creaking gate hangs longest," she said. "That means even when something doesn't look as if it's OK, it may keep going for years. And some things that look shiny and wonderful are rotten inside, so it works the other way as well."

"I suppose so," I said. "It can't be very nice."

"You're a real romantic, aren't you?" she said. "Of course it's not *nice*. But then, I couldn't honestly say that Mummy's a very *nice* person, could you?"

"Do you think it's her fault?" I asked.

"Yes," Sophie said sharply.

We had half-filled a plastic bag with a variety of winged and furred seeds. At the corner of the wood, near the fallen tree where once, two years before, we had brought a cousin of ours on a walk, we stopped and looked down on the farm.

"Do you think it's empty?" I said.

"I don't know. There's a conker tree down there," Sophie added. "They're seeds, too."

"Can we go and get some?"

"If you like. And those ones right down there are ordinary chestnuts. If we get some of those, we can eat them. We'll have a chestnut roast."

"Yeah!"

She grinned. "Come on, then. We can have a look at the farm on the way."

Even at the time, I half suspected that Sophie's real reason for cutting down across the fields was to see what had happened to the old farm, whether it had really been sold or not. We scrambled under barbed wire and over a dry-stone wall, and ended up on a winding track spanning the distance between the road and the farm buildings. The three chestnut trees were a little farther along it, the conker tree almost next to us. We spent a happy half an hour grubbing up spiky conker husks and rubbing them with our feet until they popped open to disgorge the glowing brown conkers. Quickly, I amassed a large collection in the bottom of the bag, as well as pockets full of the most impressive-looking. Then we went on down the lane to the chestnuts, and repeated the performance, only with less enthusiasm; too many of the cases revealed only wafer-thin, useless nuts. Eventually, though, we decided we had enough of these for a decent feast.

"Right," Sophie said at last. "If we go back that way, we'll have a look as we go past."

The farm buildings were low and grey. It was nowhere near

as big a farm as the one on the opposite side of the road, which had a number of big red tractors and an evil, one-eyed cat that sat on the wall and hissed. Instead, there were a couple of houses, a shed with some oil cans in it, and a long barn, made out of corrugated iron. We crept into the farmyard, and, having satisfied ourselves that there was no one around, began to explore. One of the proper buildings had its windows boarded up so that we couldn't see in, while the other—which, I guessed, had been the farmhouse proper—had been emptied. We poked around in the shed, and tried the door on the barn, but it was locked. Sophie, though, didn't seem at all disappointed.

"That's enough," she said. "We'd better get home before it gets dark. We'll go down to the quarry at the weekend and roast chestnuts; how about that?"

"Great!" I said.

"You realized far earlier than I did," he says. "About everything, I suppose. There wasn't a lot left for me to find out on my own."

I keep quiet, afraid of angering him. I had thought that the panic had worked itself out of me earlier, in the shouting and struggling before he hit me. It seems now that I was wrong; I can feel it tugging insistently at me from inside, prying me open. I swallow. I *must* keep calm, even if it is only on the outside. And I can't afford to crack up. Not now.

He is still talking. "The only thing I *did* find out was about you, and even then you practically held my hand and led me to it." He smiles. "Practically."

"You mean the—the quarry books?" I say.

He notices something different in my voice. "Sophie? Are you OK?"

"I'm fine," I say. It sounds a little crazy. Again, I have to stop myself from laughing.

"If you're sure," he says slowly. "Yes, the quarry books. That's right. I should have got them earlier, but—well, you know. There was a lot going on."

I am not at all sure that I understand what he means. I nod, encouragingly.

"I'm losing track of things," he says absently. "We found the barn. That always seems like a landmark. No, not that. A turning point. Something important." His eyes are fixed on me. "Why didn't you want things to change?"

The question takes me completely by surprise, and I answer without thinking. "Because I was scared."

He sits motionless for a long moment, and then his shoulders slump fractionally. "Yeah. That's what I thought." He sounds as if, somehow, I have disappointed him.

We stood and examined the door carefully. There was a strong-looking chain looped through the handles, padlocked twice. Sophie scratched her nose and tugged experimentally on the door.

"This is no good at all. Just as well, really. It's a bit bloody obvious to leave a door open. Let's check the sides."

We walked slowly round the barn, examining the corrugated sheeting near where it met the ground. Weeds had sprung up, and in places the metal was rusted through in holes and lines, but the structure looked secure. It was Saturday morning.

"I don't see any way in," I said.

"That's because there isn't one. Come on." She led the way over the courtyard towards the shed where the oil barrels were, scanning the place, looking for something. "This'll do." From a shelf on one side, she picked up an old and very rusty iron pipe, about two feet long. "How do you fancy a bit of breaking and entering?"

"You'll never break the chain with that," I said dubiously.

"Not the chain, stupid. The metal panels are riveted on. I think we should be able to knock the heads off the rivets." She frowned for a moment. "We could do with a chisel or something. If it doesn't work properly with this, we'll have to take the one from the quarry."

We made a second circuit of the barn. "This looks like a good place," I said.

"No use. It's on the village side. We don't want to chance being seen going in or out. It's going to have to be on the other side, facing the hill. How about this?"

I stared at the section she was indicating. "Yeah. Maybe. What do you think's inside?"

"Oh, treasure and princesses," Sophie said casually, and then burst out laughing at my expression. "Well, *honestly*, Mattie— what do you think? Some mouldy hay, if we're lucky. Come on."

With enthusiastic dedication we took it in turns to hammer at the protruding heads of the rivets. The barn, which I had expected to ring like a gong, yielded only a metallic thud every time we hit it. The first head snapped off easily, already nearly rotted through. So did the second. Then, as we progressed up the panel, they grew tougher and more resistant, until at last we reached one—at a height of about thirty inches—which we couldn't break.

"Forget it," Sophie said. "We'll do this lot next." She pointed to a parallel row two feet farther on. "If we get both lots off, we should be able to prise it back and snap the ones at the top."

Gradually, we did so. One by one, the rivet heads gave in to our incessant pounding and sheared free. Eventually, Sophie put down the piece of iron and straightened up.

"OK. What we want to do is lift it up from the bottom, like we were going to peel it up. But waggle it backwards and forwards to break that one there," she added, "and not the other one. If we leave one of the top corners attached, it will act as a sort of hinge for this panel, and hold it in place better. All right?"

"Yeah," I said. We took a bottom corner each.

"Ready?" I nodded. "Right, then. Pull."

We heaved the rusty sheet upwards, trying to avoid the sting-ing nettles and the sharper rusty edges. Then once it was out at a reasonable angle, we began to rock it back and forth, bending it a little so that the main stress was put on one of the two re-maining rivets. After three or four tries, it suddenly snapped in half with an audible crack.

"There!" I gasped. We took a step back and surveyed our new door.

"Should be pretty much invisible from ten yards away," So-phie said approvingly. "And we can bend it back to being much straighter than it is at the moment, too." She glanced at me, and grinned. "Come on. Let's see what we've got."

We swung the panel aside and scrambled through the gap on our hands and knees. Reaching outside again, Sophie dragged it back down into place, and the fan of sunlight was abruptly cut off. We stood up, and looked around us in the gloom.

"Wow," I said, still panting a little. "It's really huge."

Sophie took a step forward. "Not bad," I heard her murmur.

The inside of the barn was larger than the assembly hall at school. The floor was hard-packed earth, uneven and covered with a layer of chaff. Down one end there was a large, empty ta-ble and a pile of fertilizer sacks. Filling the remainder of the barn was a sprawling mess of bales. Two thin windows, one at each end and very high up, let in spears of light in which dust motes swirled and flowed lazily, as if they were in treacle.

"Is that hay?" I asked Sophie.

"Don't think so. It's straw, I think." She sniffed. "Probably last year's, too. God knows why it's still here. I think they would have sold hay." She took another step forward, almost hesitantly, and looked around her. "This is pretty good," she said. "You want to explore?"

"OK," I said, and made off towards the table end. There was almost nothing else worth seeing; this was the end that pointed towards our house, the end with the doors. The opposite end, pointing towards the village, was the end with the straw. The smell of the place was thick and musty, with overtones of cows and sunlight and heat. It was not unpleasant. It tickled my throat, but in an unthreatening way; not like the choking constriction that came with the dreams. I trailed back along the length of the building to where Sophie was standing on a straw bale.

"We could move these, I think," she said. "If we took an end each. I've tried one and it weighs a lot, but I reckon we could do it."

"We could build them into a castle!" I said.

"Sure could," she said, and smiled. "Better things than that, too. You could make tunnels, and roof them over with other bales, and shit like that. There's enough stuff here." She thought some more. "We're going to need torches, though, and lots of batteries," she said.

"Why?"

"Think it through. Do you think it would be a good idea to light candles in here?"

I looked at the straw. "No," I said, and giggled.

"Well, then. But if we build a closed space among all that lot, there won't be any light. I'll get some this afternoon."

"Sophie?"

"Yeah? What?" She was turning in a circle on the bale, sizing up the possibilities that existed in her new domain.

"How much money do you have?"

"Ah," she said, and grinned. "You really want to know?"

"Yes!" I said, eagerly.

"Well, it's OK to tell you, I suppose." She paused. "You *really* want to know?" she asked again, her eyes sparkling.

"Tell me!"

"A few hundred quid." She registered my shocked face with evident enjoyment. "Not bad, is it?"

"Wow," I said, lamely.

"I thought she'd notice if it was a small amount, or something uneven. But if the balance is out by hundreds, then she'll probably think she's made a mistake. I bet she doesn't have any idea about keeping track of what she spends." She smiled a small, triumphant smile. "We'll get a decent lot of batteries and a few good torches. But that's all. The rest of the money's for important things only, not sweets or comics or crap."

"Where've you hidden it?" I asked.

"Somewhere safe. Come and look at this." She set off, climbing up the bales towards the corner of the barn where they were most highly stacked. "It's going to be really something, if we get organized." She frowned. "Damn school. It should be the summer holidays. We'll have to work at it at weekends. We can always bring a picnic. Mummy's pleased if we get out of her way in any case, so that shouldn't be a problem."

I could almost sense the speed at which her mind was working, sorting out what would have to be done. In such situations, it was generally pointless my trying to volunteer anything that Sophie hadn't already thought of, so I sat down on a bale and stretched my legs out.

"We'll have to buy the torches and stuff at different shops, one at a time. Batteries, too," she was saying. "Thank God I got small notes."

I stared at the far-off roof of the barn, supported by metal girders and wooden beams. Despite the smell of cows and the dusty air, it was like a cavern out of a fairy story to me; I sat with my mouth open and my head thrown back, imagining the wonderful things we might do. There was a thump, as Sophie jumped down beside me.

"We'd better be getting home," she said. "We've been here an hour and a half, and we're going to miss lunch. We'll go shopping this afternoon for the things we need."

"Couldn't we get just *some* sweets as well? For a celebration?"

"Hmm. I suppose so."

"Great," I said with satisfaction.

# eight

"The barn confused me," he says. "I knew what it was—another secret place, like the quarry and the holly bush. But it was different to them, too public, almost. Strange. I realized afterwards, of course."

I am feeling better. For a while, now, sudden splinters of panic have been grating inside me, but they come and go. In the spaces between them, I am more settled. It had occurred to me that the unusual period of calm that came over me when Matthew started his story was perhaps shock; this makes sense. At the same time, I know that I need to hang on to it, however artificial that might seem. I can't afford not to.

These are the facts: I am a prisoner. I have looked, and looked, and I can see no simple way of escape. The man who is keeping me here I thought I knew, but I was wrong, and I am having to start afresh and learn who he is. This will take time, and I have no idea whether it will help me or not. I have no idea whether I have the time to spare. But, since there is no simple way of escape, I have determined what I am going to do. I will watch him, listen to him, get to know him as best I can. And then, maybe, I will see something that will help me. Meanwhile,

I try to keep myself from thinking that it is pointless, and I try to keep myself from crying.

I wish I were stronger.

He is saying, "Sometimes I wonder what you would have done without the barn. You would have found somewhere else, I suppose. You had that determination."

We spent nearly every evening in the barn, and much of the weekend. Over the days, with much effort, the bales of straw were stacked more and more neatly in one corner, gradually forming two sides of an enclosed space completed by the structure of the building itself. A lot of thought must have gone into planning our castle: while I had spent my daydreams imagining what games we could play in it once it was completed, Sophie had obviously turned her mind to working out how our creation should be arranged if it was to be strong and safe. There were two parts to her finished design, and since we had to build it up in layers starting at the bottom, I only realized how ingenious it was once we had finished.

The bulk of the straw was now arranged so that it walled in a comfortably large space about two thirds up its height. This could be reached by climbing up a series of short steps that Sophie had artfully concealed near the end wall of the barn itself. Once inside, you could peer out over the battlements, which included several spy-holes. The entire floor of the barn was clearly visible to the defenders of the straw castle, from the near corner down to the end where the table had been.

Sophie had moved the table first of all. It was big, made solidly from thick planks of wood, and was a good ten feet long. It took us nearly three evenings of work to shift it the length of the barn, and yet Sophie never seemed to become impatient with our lack of progress: the fact that we were still only children, which made some jobs extremely difficult, she took into account. By the time the castle was finished, the table had vanished completely, buried under bales of straw.

It preserved a hollow space deep in the centre of the castle, with the apparent main room several bales' depth above it. Moving one of the bales in the stack forming the back wall of our lookout room revealed a shaft down which you could scramble, digging your toes into the straw and holding a rope anchored at the top of the shaft. The secret door could be closed from the inside easily enough.

At the foot of the shaft we put our torches: big, rubberized models that took large square batteries.

We finished the whole project late on Saturday afternoon, one week after we had first broken into the barn. We sat in the torchlit space under the table and smiled at each other in triumph.

"It's really good," I said again. "You could hide here forever, and no one would ever know."

Sophie's smile widened. "That's right," she said. "The idea is that we use the area upstairs for most things, and keep this for anything really secret."

"Yeah!" I looked at our oak-roofed, straw-walled hideout with admiration.

Over the next couple of weeks, we slowly ferried a variety of useful items to the barn. The hidden room became furnished with a rug, and the walls were hung with a series of posters showing fighter aircraft that I had been collecting.

The torches were deployed carefully, with one in each corner of the room plus one at the top of the entrance shaft, so that you could see the rope clearly. We replaced this one on its hollowed-out shelf of straw every time we left. The rug covered the bare earth floor so that we could sit down comfortably; the roof was ample for this, but it would have been too low for us to sit on chairs or sections of log or whatever. Again, we collected bricks to serve as podiums for the torches. The smell of cows was still strong, and Sophie tackled this soon enough.

"We're going to have to be really careful," she said. "So watch. Here and here there are cans of water, OK?"

I nodded. "OK."

"And the entrance is open. It's not as though anything's likely to go wrong, but it would be a bit stupid to barbecue ourselves just because we don't like the smell." I giggled, nervously.

Sophie had bought a packet of incense sticks from the chemist in the village, and we had three of them stuck in half a potato in the middle of the floor. Deliberately, Sophie lit a match and set it to the end of each, until they were all alight. Then she dropped the match into one of the cans of water, waited a moment for the three small flames to settle, and then blew them out. We watched in silent fascination as three bright worms of light crept at almost imperceptible speed down the sticks, and a heady aromatic fragrance filled the hidden room. The smell was pervasive, powerful in the confined space. After a little while, a haze of smoke like a fog-bank began to form just below the ceiling.

Once the sticks had burnt out, Sophie dropped them into water as well. "Right. Let's shut the door and leave it to stew overnight. It should be better, I hope."

I sniffed. "Smells like cows with perfume," I said, and Sophie laughed.

"Yeah, that's about right. Come on. You bring that water tin, and go first. I'll do the other one and the torch."

At school, the lessons crawled by unmemorably. My science project on seeds won me a Mars bar and a *Well done, this is very good*, and the hybrid Spitfire edged with maddening slowness towards completion. The free activity period that our class had twice a week was spent in a crumbling annex to the Art room, amidst much secrecy. More time was spent repelling curious snoopers than actually constructing the plane. James had his plans for authentic camouflage mapped out on greaseproof paper, and had mixed a series of dirty browns and greens for the top of the body, and a pleasingly duck-egg blue for the bottom, from his older brother's collection of paints. By taking a little from each of several tins, he had managed to mix up quite a quantity of paint without his older brother noticing. In the small annex, the smells of paint oil and the nail-polish tang of dope laced the air. We had divided our tasks evenly: James was Artistic Director, Jerry was Construction—which mostly meant gluing—Simon was Chief Planner (and drew the shapes on the sheets of balsa wood) while I was Chief Engineer, doing most of the cutting with an impressive craft knife. In addition to these main posts, we all doubled as Security, protecting our brainchild from any interference. In this respect, the craft knife doubled as our Nuclear Deterrent. Most of the official names for posts and jobs were worked out by Simon. We spent the time waiting for the glue or paint or dope to dry, talking.

"My brother's got some porno magazines hidden under his mattress," James was saying. "I found them last summer. My mum would flip if she knew."

"What're they like?"

"I only got a quick look. They were pretty good," he added casually. Simon nodded, knowingly.

"I saw my cousin once," Jerry said, and paused for effect. "*Naked*. She's seventeen."

"Bullshit."

"I did! She was getting undressed."

"I think Jerry's talking bullshit," Simon said. "Serious bullshit."

"Not true. I saw her."

There was a moment's hushed silence. Then Simon whispered, in a ridiculously theatrical voice, *"Naked."* James and I exploded with laughter, howling madly. There was a thump on the door.

"Keep the noise down in there!" shouted the Art master. We stifled our giggles with difficulty.

"Anyway," Simon went on, more quietly, "how did you see her . . . *naked*?"

"Shut up," Jerry said.

"Yeah, come on," James said. "Did you really, then?"

"I told you, yeah. We were staying at my aunt's house, and I got up for a pee late at night. About eleven, I think. Maybe a bit later."

"Get *on* with it," Simon interrupted.

"Anyway, her door was a bit open, and I saw her. Then she put on a dressing gown."

We stared at him quizzically. James said, "Is that—is that it?"

"Yeah. Why?"

"What was she like?"

Simon said, "She was . . . *naked*." I hiccupped with laughter, and sat down on the edge of the table.

"Fuck off, Simon. You're such a dick sometimes."

"I think this is dry enough," James said, tapping the wing section gently. "Have we got time to do any more?"

I looked at my watch. "Not today," I said.

That weekend, the canvas bag was sodden with water, and there were wide, shallow puddles across the quarry floor. It had rained in the night, and the sky now was a dark and smoky grey.

Sophie pulled out the biscuit tin and shook the beading of water from it.

"You could put your quarry books in the barn," I said. "Then they wouldn't get wet."

"They don't get wet now, though," Sophie said, opening the tin. "See? That's what the plastic bags are for."

I rubbed my elbows and peered over her shoulder at the four or five exercise books, lying safe and dry in the tin. "I'm cold," I said.

"You can go back to the house, if you like," Sophie offered.

"No," I said, and wandered across the quarry towards the far end, where the weeds that had shot up in summer were wispy and brown in the moist air. We hadn't been to the quarry for weeks, and—strangely—I found that I was at a loss for something to do. The fossils in the rock weren't as exciting as the balsa Spitfire, and I hadn't thought to bring a book with me. Hugging my arms to myself, I considered—not for the first time—that Sophie was sometimes very strange. The quarry books I did not understand, although their constancy in my memory made them an accepted part of life. More and more, though, her trips to the quarry to scribble nonsense struck me as almost childish, an unnecessary fantasy. I swung my trainer-shod feet in narrow arcs, knocking over weed stems.

At the same time, looking back, the gap between Sophie and me might even have narrowed a little. At the age of nine, I was a stage more responsible, a stage less vulnerable, and Sophie did not have to devote as much time to looking after me. Often we might do different things for an evening, although we'd always end up meeting at bedtime. There was more space between us, and this brought us fractionally closer together.

● ● ●

He gets up, walks—a little unsteadily—across the room to the window. This time, however, he appears not to be looking out through the cracks in the boards, but studying his own reflection in the dark glass. A draught stirs his hair slightly. Without looking at me, he asks, "Did you feel that, too?"

"The drawing together?"

"Mm." He rests his elbows on the windowsill. "I think I did, even then. I only put it into words later, of course; but then, that's true of a lot of this. You don't realize at the time how much you *do* understand. It's all there, but you can't express it. Well, I couldn't, anyway. You were different."

"Isn't that true of everyone?"

"Yeah. Mostly. But you *needed* to express what you felt, to let it out somehow. And there was no one there to listen to you."

"You were there," I say, tentatively.

I can hear from his voice that he is smiling. "But you didn't really tell me, did you? You knew I wouldn't understand."

"Do you now?"

"Yes." He hesitates. "No. I'm not sure. I thought I understood everything, at one point. But—since then, well, things have changed. . . ."

He trails off, and I am left silently agreeing with him: things *have* changed. It crosses my mind to wonder when, exactly, it was that he thought he understood everything. There's so much that he's not telling me yet.

Eventually, he says, "Sometimes, it seems like I spent my childhood finding out about my childhood. If you see what I mean."

"Yes," I say. "I see exactly."

Miss Finch was our form teacher and our History teacher, a steely haired lady with a sharp tongue and a keen sense of justice. Of all the teachers I knew, I liked Miss Finch best, if only because she was guaranteed to be fair in dealing with any problem, and also because she seemed to show a genuine interest in her pupils. We had been working through the basic curriculum requirements of our History course for the first part of the term, and, as half-term approached, Miss Finch called a halt to the mundane work and announced something different.

"It's a week or so before half-term," she said, addressing the whole class. "I know some of you will have work to take home, and I don't want to give you too much to do. It's good to have a break. But," she went on, as one or two people exchanged hopeful grins, "I would like to give you a short project to do. It doesn't have to be long; it's more a mini-project, and you can do it fairly much as you like. If you worked hard, you could have it finished before half-term begins. Now, I'm going to call you up one by one and we'll discuss what you might like to have a go at. The rest of the class can continue with what we started yesterday."

I bent back over my work and looked at it carefully. Before long, my name was called, and I went up to Miss Finch's desk.

"Hello, Matthew," she said. She always used our full names—one thing about her that I didn't like. "I was quite pleased by the story you did for homework."

"Thank you," I said.

"Now, what I think you should be doing with this project is finding out about something—or someone—new, try to tackle something you haven't done before. How does that sound?"

"OK."

"I heard in the staffroom that you're building an aeroplane. Is that right?"

I blinked, surprised by the change of tack. "Yeah. Me and Simon are making it in our activities period."

"Simon and *I*," Miss Finch said, with a small smile. "It sounds like fun. So I thought perhaps you'd like to do a project on this man." She slid a photocopy across to me. "Do you know who he is?"

"No," I admitted.

"Well, he's called Leonardo da Vinci. He spent a lot of time building things as well. Not aeroplanes, although he designed some interesting flying machines. He was born in 1452."

"He did that painting," I said. "The *Mona Lisa*."

Miss Finch looked slightly surprised. "That's right, he did. And as well as being an artist, he was a scientist and an engineer and a few other things as well. He's probably one of the most interesting people in history. Now, I know there's a lot to say about someone like this, but I thought you could concentrate on his flying machines. I had a look through this book earlier, and there's a parachute, and a sort of helicopter, and several sketches of strap-on wings."

She passed me a large book, illustrated in colour. "You can borrow that over half-term, but make sure it comes back in one piece. What do you think?"

"It sounds great," I said, and I actually meant it. Miss Finch must have realized, because she smiled warmly.

"Good. It's supposed to be a fun project, so concentrate on the things you really find interesting. You can take the book with you. Who's next? Vivien Jenkins! Your turn."

I went back to my desk with the book, and, once seated, leafed through it with interest. There were lots of photos and pictures, models of some of da Vinci's inventions, diagrams of how others might have looked. There was a sort of tank, and a thing with flails attached to it.

I turned the page. There was a photograph of one of his original sketches, on browny-yellow paper, surrounded by dense writing. I squinted at the lines closely, but they didn't seem to make sense. Puzzled, I stared harder. They were almost like something else.

The asthma attack took me completely by surprise. It was so sudden that it felt as though someone had stuffed cotton wool into my throat and chest. For a long moment I had no idea what to do, and then I remembered the inhaler in my desk. Pushing the lid up cascaded the book and the paper I had been working on onto the floor, and Miss Finch looked up sharply. I clutched the inhaler and slapped it to my mouth, triggering the release automatically. There was another long pause, and the sounds of the classroom seemed to have become much farther away. The desk in front of me, where my eyes had fixed, had started to tinge with red around the edges. I could see Miss Finch coming towards me across the classroom, but her movements were slowed and distorted. I triggered the inhaler a second time, but couldn't even tell if I had managed to breathe in any of the spray.

Miss Finch was beside me, trying to help. I felt her push the nozzle of the inhaler more firmly into my mouth, and heard her shout something into my ear, her tone imperative. Obediently, I sucked as hard as I could, and finally the red haze cleared from my vision.

Gradually, I found that I was able to exhale properly again. For a long time I sat there, my chest heaving as I struggled to stop trembling. Tears had run inadvertently down my face, and the classroom was hushed. Gently, Miss Finch prised my hand away from my face and set the inhaler down on the desk.

"How do you feel?" she asked quietly.

"OK, I think," I said. The words sounded harsh, as if something had been torn in my voice.

She nodded. "Do you want some water?"

"No thanks."

"Well." She straightened up just as the bell rang for the next lesson. "Charlotte? Can you tell your next teacher that Matthew Howard may be a little late? Thank you." The classroom drained of children until we were left alone. There was the sound of feet and talking in the passage outside.

"Well," said Miss Finch again. "What on earth brought that on? You were fine a minute ago."

"I don't know," I said. "It sometimes happens like that."

"Have you seen a doctor about it?"

"Yes," I said. "That's why I have the inhaler."

"I meant recently," she replied. "Have you seen a doctor in the last six months?"

"Uh, no," I said.

"Where do you get your inhalers, then?"

"Mummy gets them for me," I said.

Her lips compressed slightly. "I'll call your mother and suggest you have a checkup," she said.

"All right," I agreed miserably. There was no point whatsoever arguing with Miss Finch.

"Now, do you feel you can go to your next lesson? If you're at all worried, I'll take you up to Mr. Fergus and you can go home."

I thought about the idea of going home. "I'm OK," I said. "I think it's stopped now."

Miss Finch looked dubious. "Well, if you're sure," she said. Then, with more of her usual decisiveness, she swept together the scattered papers and put them on my desk along with the book. "You'd better get along," she said. "I'll put this away for you. Don't forget to say sorry you're late."

"I won't," I said, standing a little queasily. Then, fighting down a brief pounding of my heart, I said, "Miss Finch?"

"Yes?"

I opened the book to the right page. "Why can't I read this?"

She glanced at the page. "You really *are* feeling better, aren't you? That's good news. I think you had us all a bit worried back there." She smiled. "Let's see. Oh, right. Well, for a start, Leonardo was Italian, so you can't read it because it's in a different language."

"Is that all?"

She looked at me, and there was something strange in her expression. "No, actually. It's written back to front and inside out—like mirror-writing, you see. Leonardo didn't want anyone to read his notes, so he invented this as a sort of code."

"So no one would understand it?"

"That's right. It's all in the book, if you read it."

"I will," I promised.

When school that day was over, Sophie met me at the gate and we started to walk home together. Under my arm I clutched a ring-binder file and the book Miss Finch had given me. I was subdued, for any number of reasons, with thoughts streaming through my mind too quickly to analyse properly.

"You're quiet," Sophie observed.

"Mm."

"Anything wrong?"

"I had an asthma attack in History," I said.

"Yeah?"

"Miss Finch said she was going to phone Mummy and say I should go to the doctor."

Sophie nodded thoughtfully. "I see. And?"

"I don't know." I sighed. "I don't want Mummy to be cross."

"Hey," she said, concerned. "Don't worry about it. It'll be all right." Her tone wasn't as light as it could have been, though, and I didn't feel any better. "Anything else happen?"

"I'm going to do a project on Leonardo da Vinci," I said.

"Oh, right. The painter."

"He was really clever," I said, looking sideways to catch any reaction. "He—designed lots of things, like tanks and stuff."

"That's right. How's the plane going?"

"It's going OK," I said. "I don't know if it'll be ready by half-term. How long is there to go?"

"Not this weekend, but next weekend."

"We've done the wings," I added, "But they weren't too difficult."

"I'm really looking forward to seeing this grand project once it's done," Sophie said.

"Yeah?"

"Yeah."

When we got home, Sophie went upstairs. I found some squash in the kitchen and made myself a drink.

"Matthew," my mother said from the doorway. "Would you come with me, please. There's something I want to talk to you about."

She seemed quite calm. I set the glass down and followed her to the drawing room, shrugging my shoes off at the door as usual. Mummy had walked at first as if to take her normal place in the high-backed armchair, but at the last moment she stopped, and turned, and went instead over to the window. Outside, there was a limited view of the lawn and back garden, to only about a quarter of the way down. My mother stood with her back to me for a long time, haloed with light from the single window of the otherwise dark room.

Finally, still staring outside, she said, "I had a call from a Miss Fitch this afternoon, Matthew. Do you know her?"

"Uh, Miss Finch," I said. "She's my form teacher." I could feel a tightening in my chest already, and fought it down as best I could.

"This—" Mummy paused. "This Miss Fitch says you had some sort of attack in her lesson. Is that right?"

"Yes," I said miserably. "I—"

"Thank you. Be quiet." She exhaled harshly. "Matthew, I realize that sometimes a subject can be boring. I haven't forgotten what it was to be at school myself."

"I don't—"

"Be quiet, please." She turned to face me at last. "But I will not have you—*disgracing* yourself like this, just to get attention. Do you understand?"

I looked at her blankly.

"Answer me," she said, softly.

"Yes."

"So. You understand what you have been doing, and yet you did it anyway. Is that it?" The smell of dust grew stronger, and I felt my chest tighten, almost imperceptibly.

"I—"

"Don't think I don't know about you, Matthew. Everything about you." She took a shuddering breath. "You're like your father. All you care about is you, you, you. And never think of *me*, perhaps? Isn't that the way of it?"

Her voice had got louder. I shook my head dumbly, but she hardly seemed to notice. Her gaze was fixed somewhere past me, her eyes failing to take me in. I was frightened.

"I know *everything*," she said again. "Stains on the bedclothes. Do you think I never noticed?"

I opened my mouth, but no sound came out.

"*My* fucking bedclothes!" she shouted, and the force of the shout rocked me back on my heels for a moment. "You bastard, I even know who she was, did you realize that? I know where she lived. The whore's apartment. Did you soil her sheets as well, mark out your territory like an animal?"

"Hello, Mummy," Sophie said. My mother's head jerked back as if she'd been slapped, and she closed her mouth. The abrupt silence in the room lengthened horribly. Sophie, standing just inside the doorway, was watching my mother with a level, almost sad expression. At last, my mother's breath seemed to find the force to escape her body.

"Take off your shoes," she said, and the words were almost a whisper. "This is the drawing room. Take them off."

"I think that's enough, don't you?" Sophie replied. "Matthew and I are going out to play. We'll get our own supper."

My mother crumpled into her armchair as if Sophie's gaze had eroded her insides. "Take off your fucking shoes," she muttered, but she no longer seemed to be talking to us.

"C'mon, Mattie," Sophie said, and took me gently by the hand. Over her shoulder, she said, "You know *nothing*, Mummy. Remember that." We closed the drawing room door carefully behind us.

Once we were upstairs, she said, "You OK?"

"Yeah," I said, a little unsteadily. "What was she talking about?"

"Things that happened a long time ago. Nothing to do with you." Sophie stroked my hair back from my eyes and smiled sadly. "Ignore her. You're quite safe. She makes a lot of noise, I know, but there's nothing she can do anymore."

"Really?"

"Really. I promise. That's all over now."

"I was scared," I said. "I don't understand what she was saying. All Miss Finch did was phone up—"

"Ssh," Sophie said. "I know. It's not your fault." We sat on the edge of my bed together, and when I looked at her, Sophie's eyes were fixed on some distant inner landscape that I would never see.

# nine

I had thought that I knew Matthew, but now I am getting to know him a second time. His quirks, his habitual movements, his turns of phrase—I watch them all with the intent fascination that comes as a part of fear. At the moment, there's no one else that matters.

I keep returning to ideas of escape. They're all impractical. There is nowhere nearby that I could get to, even if I somehow managed to leave this room. The farm down the road is a mile or more away, and as deserted as this place. I'm fully aware that there's no point in thinking the same things again and again, but I can't help myself. The moment I stop concentrating on what is actually in front of me, my mind turns immediately to dreams of running away from here, leaving him alone in the house with his candles and memories. I am constantly trying not to do this. There is a conviction building in me that the way to escape is buried in what he is saying, if I can only trace it through the knots and tangles of his story. I feel it. If I can piece together the past, the present will take care of itself.

I hope I am right. It sounds easy enough, but sometimes I worry that I am just comforting myself, that somewhere along the line my brain has realized there's nothing I can do, and is just attempting to keep me calm. I don't know. I feel that I'm playing tricks on myself.

Strangely, though, Matthew's story is itself helping me. Not just in the way I've described—giving me more details of him and his past—but also in another way. It lets me see the Sophie of Matthew's childhood through his eyes. And, whether he likes it or not, no matter what he tells me and himself about his being in control now, I know that when he looks at me, some portion of that little girl is still evident in what he sees. I thought at first that this was dangerous to me, but I have started to think that I was wrong, that in fact it may be a weapon to use against him. I am sure he doesn't see it like this. He may not even be aware of it. It doesn't matter; when I see a way that it might be used, I have it ready.

It occurs to me suddenly, in the middle of thinking all this, that he may be justified; after all, what else am I doing but keeping secrets, trying to hide the truth, plotting against him? It's almost as if he were right about everything.

In another place, that thought would be amusing, but not here. I draw my legs up further, knees pushing against my chest, and hug my arms around my shins. The tape has twisted a little, cutting into my wrists, but I put up with it. It is another device with which to remind myself that I have to keep trying.

He says, "What are you thinking?"

I blink. "What?"

"You look like you're thinking."

"I was thinking about the barn," I say.

He nods. "Yeah. Me too." He scratches the side of his neck, looking up at the ceiling.

• • •

On Sunday morning, we set off late. The sun was large and pale above the hills beyond the wood, hanging in the sky behind a misty wash of thin cloud. The air was still, and the colours of the wood were even more splendid than they had been the evening before when we had walked home. We took the path up from the end of the garden until we were about halfway to the top of the quarry hill, and then cut through the broken wall and across the empty fields. Crows scattered away from us lethargically, and the grey and rust-coloured buildings of the deserted farm grew slowly larger. It was cold, the invigorating tang of the coming winter tempered with the rich smells and flavours of autumn earth and leaf mold, bonfire smoke and fallen apples. We scrambled into the lane near the chestnut and conker trees.

The section of corrugated iron turned smoothly on its remaining rivet now, where Sophie had dripped oil on to it. We held it for one another as we scuffed our way inside. The inside of the old barn was shadowy and cool, catching both light and heat more readily at midday and in the afternoon. I ran down its length to the far end, enjoying the emptiness of the space, while Sophie climbed up into the castle.

"Mattie?"

"Yeah?" I called back.

"Come here a minute, would you?"

I ran back, pleased that I was barely breathing hard, and followed her until I could poke my head over the battlements and look into the upper room. "What?"

She nodded at the scattered crayons and paper and stuff. "You didn't touch anything, did you?"

"No," I said.

"You're really sure? You didn't kick something by accident?"

"No. I don't play near there in any case. I play over here."

"Yeah, I remember."

"Why? Is something changed?"

She looked at the childish debris steadily. I followed her gaze, and couldn't see that anything was any different to the last time we were here. "Yes," she said. "Yes, it's changed. Someone's been here."

Abruptly, the sense of fun was gone from the atmosphere. I realized that we had no way of knowing who the stranger might be. "What—I mean, do you think they'll come back?" I asked.

"I don't know," Sophie said. "Come on. We'd better get things ready."

The thrill of excitement and fear at finding that someone else knew about the barn, and had been there, made me eager to help Sophie prepare everything the way she wanted it. First of all, she checked the secret room, made sure that nothing in there was disturbed.

Presently she reported, "No, nothing's moved. So they only know about the upstairs room, which is fine. Even so, it's going to be difficult." She paused, thoughtfully. "We can assume they're kids, because adults wouldn't bother climbing the bales or messing around with the stuff. Which means they'll probably be back."

"When?" I asked.

"I should think today," Sophie said. "After all, it's the weekend, and they'll have school or whatever in the week. First things first, though. We need to be somewhere else."

So saying, she led the way out of the barn. The sunlight made me blink after the gloom; Sophie scanned the farm quickly. "I don't see anyone. You?"

"No," I said.

"Right. We need somewhere that we can see the barn from easily, and not be seen ourselves. Let's get back into the lane."

We climbed the dry-stone wall but this time, instead of going down towards the chestnut trees, we walked up the hill a little way until the scraggy hedge that augmented the wall was thicker. Here, we stopped, commanding a fair view of the farm court-yard and the side of the barn with our doorway in it.

"We'll take turns at guard duty," Sophie said. "Just watch through the hedge and see if anyone turns up. Do you want a sandwich?"

"All right. What sort is it?"

"Ham and cheese."

We watched the barn in quarter of an hour shifts, talking about school and people in the meantime. The sun was a little warmer now that it was nearly midday; from the other side of the village, in the middle distance, I could see the plume of smoke from a bonfire drifting lazily up before being dispersed by invisible currents of air.

Sophie sat on the wall and swung her feet thoughtfully.

"Still no one?"

"No," I confirmed. "When do you think they'll come?"

"Well, they might not come today at all," she admitted. "It seems more likely, though. And I don't want to be inside the barn when they arrive; I want us to see them first."

"Then what do we do?" I asked.

"That depends on who it is," Sophie said. "We may have to abandon the barn."

"We could make a club, and let them join," I said, thinking of the model aeroplane group.

"Yeah, something like that," she said vaguely. "We'll see."

We waited until one o'clock, and still there was no sign of anyone.

"I'm bored," I said. "How much longer do we have to wait?"

"What do you want to do instead?"

"I don't know," I said. "Go up to the woods?"

Sophie shrugged. "OK. Leave the sandwich box on the wall there, we'll pick it up later."

The woods towards which we headed were beyond the field at the top of the lane; over to our left, a few fields' distance away, was the clearing with the fallen tree. We carried on straight up, though, until we found ourselves pushing through the unruly growth of saplings and bushes that formed the outskirts of the wood. Further in, the ground cover thinned out a bit, until we were walking on a deep cushion of fallen leaves, the top layer still crisp and brown as if they had been deep fried. I kicked leaves up and scuffed my feet to leave trails behind me, and Sophie laughed and did likewise. There were alarmed calls from birds deeper in the wood, and high above us, the nests of rooks were scattered through the high branches.

Toadstools glistened at the roots of some of the trees. In the pocket of my anorak were a couple of toy aircraft, but I didn't bother playing with them; there was no need. A horse-chestnut tree yielded up some rather soggy conkers, which I hurled at toadstools, making them spatter into startlingly white pieces. The air felt thin and clean.

We spent a good hour or so in the woods, walking in a wide circle that brought us out nearly where we had started. As we set off back down the lane once more, I rolled the roundest stones down in front of us, to see how far they would go. The white square of the lunch box was just visible on the wall when Sophie put her hand out to stop me.

"Hang on," she said. "Look."

I followed her pointing finger. Down in front of us, in the courtyard of the empty farm, were two figures in brightly coloured anoraks. As we watched, they moved about aimlessly for a while, going up to the boarded windows and examining them, poking around in the shed where the oil drums were, and finally coming round to the near side of the barn. There was a pause then, as they tried to identify the loose sheet of metal; after a couple of unsuccessful tries, they found it, and slipped inside.

"Well," Sophie said. "There we go. Come on, let's get closer."

We ran down the slope as far as the thicker section of hedge and stopped there, peering intently at the blank side of the barn. We could hear nothing, and there was nothing visible to indicate that anything was amiss.

"What do we do now?" I said.

"I want to know who they are," Sophie said. She seemed to be thinking for a moment, and then she said, "Stay here. I'm going to have a look—shan't be long."

I stared after her as she scrambled over the wall and headed down towards the farm below.

Sophie was gone for nearly a quarter of an hour. After ten minutes had passed, I grew worried, not certain what might have happened. I'd seen her walk around the perimeter of the barn, pause at one point to put her face close to the metal as if peering through a hole, and then go around to the entrance and crawl inside. After that, there had been no movement, no sound. I was growing agitated and nervous, wondering if I should follow her down, when the panel slid aside again. My heart leapt in my throat as one of the strangers—this one in a red anorak—came out. Then, after a moment, the other followed. A sudden panic seized me that Sophie was not going to come out at all, but then I saw her smaller figure straighten up in the shadow of the barn. Then the three of them stood for a while—talking, I supposed— before splitting up. Sophie started out across the field that would bring her back to me, while the two strangers cut across to join the lane farther down, near the main road. I waited impatiently for her to reach me.

"What's happened?" I demanded. "Who were they?"

"Hang on a minute, for heaven's sake. I'll tell you everything once I've got my breath back." She sat down on the top of the wall and swung her feet. "Right. Like we thought, they're kids. Older than us." A curious expression came over her face. "One of them's thirteen and the other's fifteen. Ah . . . they're called Andrew and Steven." She smiled, almost. "You remember getting beaten up at school? About a couple of years ago?"

"No," I said, puzzled.

"Yes you do. We got the rest of the day off 'cos I broke a tooth."

"Oh, yeah," I said. "That was *you* that got beaten up."

"You do remember. Well, Andrew of the barn is also Andrew of the playground bullying—the one they kicked out. And Steven's his older brother."

I didn't know what to say. The details of the incident, two years previously, had faded and become smudged in my mind. I wasn't even sure I could remember the faces of the boys involved, and besides, once they'd left the school, they had vanished from my life so utterly I hadn't given them a second thought. I'd certainly never expected to see either of them again.

I said, "Do they—I mean, does he remember you? What he did to you?"

Sophie's curious expression became more noticeable. "Yeah, he certainly does. But time changes people, you know. I don't think he's . . . still bullying people, if that's what worries you." She yawned casually. "In fact, I thought it would be fun if we all got together some time. They're around on Wednesday, so we'll meet up then."

"I thought you wanted the barn to be a special place?" I said, rather astonished.

"Yeah, but that doesn't mean we can't have friends round. And you said something about a club, right?" she added brightly, as if she'd just remembered it.

"I suppose so," I said.

"Great. It'll be good to have some people to talk to. You'll like Andrew, probably. And Steven's OK as well." She brushed loose hair out of her eyes. "I think I've had enough of this. Want to go to the quarry for a while?"

Remembering Leonardo, and my resolution to get a closer look at the quarry books, I nodded assent. "Yeah, that would be OK."

He looks at me, almost accusingly. "Tell me about the barn," he says.

"What do you want to know?" I say, hoping for more time.

"Just tell me why you chose it."

It is a challenge; I can see that clearly now. A test. Instinctively, I think I may be able to answer; I remind myself of what he sees me as. Why the barn?

I have it, and at the same moment I know I am right. "It was a trap," I say, trying to keep the fierce pleasure out of my voice. "Too public to be a secret place, Mattie. But safe from adults. Very specialized. The only sort of people who'd want a place like that would be—"

"People like you," he finishes. "People with something to hide." His voice is extremely quiet, almost a whisper, but his eyes seem stronger than ever. "You set it up. So casually, too. It was never even supposed to be like the quarry."

"No," I agree.

He rubs his face. "Shit." There's a pause. Then he says, "You called me Mattie."

"I did?" I can't remember. Perhaps I did. Only because he keeps calling himself that.

"Yes, you did." His eyes sparkle in the candlelight. "Strange. Some things never change."

"That's not what you said," I say. Abruptly I am scared, not at all certain where the conversation has just gone. I can feel us brushing past things that I don't understand. "You said that time changes things."

He laughs softly. "Oh, very good, Sophie. Very good. But that's not what I said; it's what *you* said. So cut out the fucking game-playing, will you? I'm not a kid anymore. And I know you."

I nod dumbly. He hasn't raised his voice, but for the first time since he hit me I am afraid for my life.

After a long while, he says, "So. Let's get back to it all." I find that I am shivering uncontrollably.

Scrambling down the shallow side of the quarry, the loose scree kept slipping out from under our feet; it was slick with rainwater from the night before. The brown weeds at one end were even more ragged, while, at the other, there were trails of stain marring the rock just below the bars of the cages. Sophie went to get the quarry bag, while I feigned lack of interest, throwing stones into the weeds and wandering about aimlessly.

After a while, Sophie returned and set the bag down on a large rock. Still casually, I went over to join her, squatting down and picking through the old fossils in the bag. She looked at me—I thought I saw curiosity in the look—and I said, "When we've finished the plane, I could launch it from over there. From the top." I pointed to the rim of the quarry above the cages.

Apparently satisfied, Sophie nodded. "Yeah, why not? If it does crash, though, you're going to fuck up your plane pretty badly." She opened the biscuit tin, took out the plastic bag with the books in, and opened it.

"What are you writing today?" I asked, knowing that I would only get half a reply.

"Just things," she said. "What's happened. You know."

"Yeah." I got up and wandered away again, feeling my stomach turn queasy. I still hadn't had a look at the quarry books, but it was important that I didn't show too much interest. It was also important that I didn't show too little; being with Sophie had attuned me to the correct way of lying, and I was surprised—and vaguely pleased—to notice that she hadn't seen anything odd. She was bent over the book, scribbling away in Biro, as I walked round the perimeter of the quarry as slowly as I could. I watched the sky, tried to think about the balsa Spitfire, *anything* to keep myself looking as I usually did. The problem was that I had no real idea of how I usually looked, while Sophie would know only too well. I turned and ambled back the way I'd come, aching to move faster, not daring to. I picked up stones and threw them, hummed songs from the radio. Eventually I decided it was enough; if I waited much longer, Sophie would finish up and the books would be put away. It occurred to me that I could always come back on my own, look at the quarry books at my leisure: but I dismissed the thought at once. The walk up to the top of the quarry hill was not really a long one—five or ten minutes, at the most—but the little path worn to the side of the dry-stone wall was exposed to view from our house, and if Sophie saw me, she would know where I was going. On top of this, although I had often replaced the bag for her at the end of a quarry afternoon, she always packaged up the books in their biscuit tin herself. What if there was some secret way of folding the plastic bag, or some particular scratch on the tin lid that had to be lined up? The possibilities were too numerous to consider.

I stopped by her shoulder. "I'm bored," I said. "Are you nearly finished? I want to go to see the barn."

"Nearly finished," she agreed. She completed the line she had been writing with a funny slash mark and looked up at me. "Why don't you go and see what the view's like from your launchpad? See if it's suitable? I'll join you in a bit."

"OK," I agreed. The letters themselves were normal, but there were funny symbols like the slash mark, and the order of the letters made no sense. They were in evenly spaced blocks, as well, which didn't look anything like normal words. "I'll wave when I'm there."

"Right." She bent back over her work and I turned and left. I was trying to remember whether the quarry books had always looked the way they did now; it seemed to me that they hadn't, that there had been a time when the strange scribbles looked more like normal words, only muddled and nonsensical. But I'd first seen the quarry books—when? When I was much younger, certainly. Perhaps as young as four, I hazarded; after all, they were so much a part of my life when I was five that I couldn't remember a time without them. I worked my way carefully up the uneven slope towards the top of the quarry, watching where I put my feet among the loose shale. Perhaps the quarry books had changed. It didn't seem to be unreasonable. Sophie was older, after all. Leonardo's quarry-writing was very different— his was mirror-writing, Miss Finch had said—but I could see easily enough that the principle was identical, even if the method wasn't. Leonardo had wanted to keep his inventions secret. Sophie's secrets were probably very different, but her reasons were the same: she didn't want anyone else to know. Out of breath, I reached the top of the quarry and paused to take a dose of the inhaler I kept in my pocket.

By this time of the autumn, the quarry was rimmed with golds and coppers, the trees that normally fringed its edges turning to the colour of beaten metals. There was a deep layer of husks and fallen leaves on the ground where I ducked down under the barbed wire and made my way outside the fence that rimmed the quarry. The very edge was crumbling a little, and, as you came up the path from the quarry floor, you could see where the rock had fallen away and there was a protruding rim of packed earth, about a foot thick, that was unsupported from below. For these reasons, the plane launch would have to be made from about four or five feet back. I walked round through the woods until I was at the right place, and then pushed through the bushes to the fence, looking for a gap or a place to climb over. I found it easily enough, where a branch had fallen and brought the tangle of wire and grey boards to the ground. I stepped through carefully, and edged forward until I could see the floor of the quarry. For a few seconds it was empty, and then Sophie appeared, walking away from my vantage point towards the exit. She had been out of sight, replacing the quarry bag near the cages beneath me.

The thought of the cages made me shudder; wherever they went, it was somewhere in the rock under my feet.

"Hi!" I called out. Sophie stopped, turned, and waved silently at me before starting up the path. I backed cautiously away from the edge and went round to meet her. All the time, a tiny, triumphant voice inside me was exultant: it was nothing much, just a glimpse at the quarry books, but I had found out a weakness in Sophie. She didn't believe that I could fool her, and I could, because she had taught me how.

•  •  •

He lapses into silence, leaving me with the last words he spoke running through my head. It's ironic; Matthew, as a child, carefully gleans fragments of information about Sophie, gradually building up a better picture of this girl that he knows but doesn't know. And now, years later, everything is reversed, and it is he who is under scrutiny, he whose every move is studied and appraised. And for much the same reasons.

# ten

Wednesday came, and when we arrived home after school, Sophie began at once to change into her jeans and anorak. There was a fine drizzle falling outside, and the day was cold.

"Where are you going?"

She grinned. "Short memory, you have. Back to the barn. We said we'd meet Andy and Steve there today."

"Oh, yeah," I said.

"I've spoken to Mummy," she added. "We can take tea with us."

"Really?"

She nodded. "Get a coat on, for heaven's sake. You can't go out like that."

"OK," I agreed, and ran upstairs, wondering how it was that Sophie could extract concessions from my mother so easily.

We reached the barn first, as Sophie had intended. "Don't let on about the second room," she warned. "That's still just for us. We'll sit up here and wait." We settled ourselves on bales of straw in the upper, open room of our straw fortress, and talked about school for a while.

After half an hour or so, there was a clatter from the metal sheeting and we both fell silent. The panel swung aside, and a hunched figure in a red anorak squeezed through.

"Shit," I heard him say. "I think I cut my hand."

"Get inside," someone else said. "It's cold out here."

The second figure followed and straightened up.

"Anyone here?"

Sophie stood up and jumped over the wall of the fort. "Yeah. Hi. I've got Mattie with me today," she said. "He's nine but he's OK."

The older boy laughed. "You sound pretty cocky," he said.

"She's always cocky," the other one said. Neither of them sounded very confident, though, and I felt some of the tension that had gathered in my chest dissipate. Try as I might, I couldn't remember either of these boys, and yet the younger one—who must be Andy—was the one who had hurt Sophie at school.

"Come on up," she said. They followed her awkwardly up the series of little steps until they were all in the upper room, looking about them diffidently.

"This is OK," Andy said. "You do this yourself?"

"No," Sophie replied. "It was all pretty much like this when we found the place. We shifted one or two of the bales to make that wall. They're pretty heavy."

"You're pretty small, that's all," the older boy—Steven—said. He was grinning.

"Shut up," Andy said uncomfortably. "It's OK." I realized, with insight that was unusual for me, that he had known Sophie for longer than Steven, and I wondered immediately what he was feeling right now. When Sophie spoke, though, she sounded neither tense nor affronted.

"Sit down," she said. "It's a bit rough, but so what."

"How'd you find this place?" Andy asked.

"Just lucky, I suppose," Sophie said. "It's empty."

"No shit," Steven said. He took a pack of cigarettes out of his pocket and lit one, throwing the spent match over the side of the fort.

"You're going to have to watch that, in here," Sophie said quietly. "I can think of nicer ways to die."

"Why, are you scared?" Steven said, grinning. There was a pause, and then Sophie grinned back.

"Can you smell burning?" she asked.

"Don't be stupid. I blew it out."

"You didn't," she said. "You waved it, but it didn't go out. Now who's stupid?"

I was watching this with wide eyes. When Sophie had spoken, I hadn't been able to smell anything, but now it seemed that she was right; there was the faintest scent of burning straw in the air. I glanced at Andy, and by his expression I guessed he could smell it, too.

"Bullshit," Steven said, but he sounded less sure.

"I can smell smoke," Sophie said. "If we sit here much longer, we're not going to be able to get down." She was speaking calmly, but there was just the right note of urgency in her voice to make it authentic. Abruptly, the smell of smoke in my nostrils died, became just the smell of straw and wet clothing. But I could see that Steven was smelling it now, and I could see that he was starting to believe.

"Shit, Steve," Andy muttered. "I can smell it, too—"

"It's bullshit," Steven said, but he was standing up even as he said it, and there was ill-concealed panic in his eyes. "I blew it out—"

He crossed to the parapet and leant out over it, scanning the straw below.

Sophie grinned. "Just a joke," she said. "You *did* blow it out. Really."

There was a long silence. Steven turned round slowly and looked at her. For a moment, I thought he was going to hit her, and I knew that there was not a thing I could do to stop him.

"Steve—" Andy said again, and Steve laughed briefly.

"Pretty good, for a twelve-year-old," he said, and the tension was gone as easily as that. He gave Sophie a curious glance, and then sat down again. I noted with interest that Sophie had gained a year in age somewhere along the way, but neither I nor Andy remarked on it, although Andy—if he had thought— should have realized that she was still only eleven, and would be for a good nine months yet.

"Yeah," Sophie agreed, crossing her legs and smiling. "I would have thought Andy would have told you that."

Steve nodded. "OK."

"So, tell us about yourselves, Steve and Andy," she said.

They looked at one another quickly. "What do you want to know?" Andy asked.

"What brought you out here?"

Steve answered. "I heard the place was empty, so we came up—just to see what was around, you know."

"Throw a few stones, break a few windows?" Sophie said sweetly.

"That's kids' stuff," he replied flatly. "No, just looking for somewhere a bit private. I thought we might be able to get into one of the farm buildings. I think you could get into several pretty easily, if you wanted to, but I reckon they'll be keeping an eye on them."

"They're pretty obvious targets," Sophie agreed. "So what do you get up to that you need your privacy so much?"

Steve laughed. "Nothing that would interest you," he said. "Your brother doesn't have a lot to say for himself, does he? Hey, you—do you talk?"

"Yes," I muttered.

Sophie said, "One thing. Don't fuck with Mattie, OK? Talk to Andy afterwards and he'll give you some reasons why not." She shot a glittering smile at Andy. "I'm older now," she said.

"Yeah, all right, I understand," Steve said, shaking his head. "Christ. You talk like a teacher, for God's sake."

"Something like that," Sophie said. "Anyway, you're more than welcome round here. We don't mind sharing."

"Yeah, sure. What if I decide I don't want you around?"

Sophie looked at him, and then smiled. "You're pretty bright," she said. "I think we'll get along OK."

"Shit," Steve said disgustedly. "I really don't believe this." He ground out the cigarette on the sole of his shoe; I noticed that he did so very carefully. Sophie's smile widened a little.

"We'll see you at the weekend, OK?" she said. "Saturday."

We watched them out of the door in silence. When the metal sheet had dropped back into its place, Sophie leant back in the straw and grinned at me.

"This is going to be really good," she said.

Friday school was chaotic, and by four o'clock teachers and pupils alike were glad to be finally heading for the gates. Sophie met me at the side of the playground and we walked home together as usual. She seemed elated about something, although she didn't mention anything particularly exciting when we were chatting about our day. I supposed that she was looking forward to meeting up with Andy and Steven again.

It is perhaps curious that I felt no jealousy, however slight, that Sophie was taking so much interest in other people; I was quietly certain that, had it been I who had suddenly decided to spend time with new friends, Sophie would have reacted differently. But a part of me even felt something like relief that Sophie's attention was being diverted a little.

That evening, I made myself a glass of squash and wandered out into the garden with it. It was cold; there was a damp smell in the air; overlaid with the smell of a bonfire. I wandered down towards the stream and the orchard, and was pleased to see that the bonfire was in our garden: a tall, neat pile of leaves and branches, smouldering damply like a sulking volcano. The evening light had started to darken, and the trees cast long shadows across the lawn. When I got back, the kitchen was empty. Upstairs, I found Sophie lying on her bed kicking one foot in the air.

"Hi," she said. "Where've you been?"

"Walking round the garden," I said. "It's starting to get dark really early."

"Yeah, that'll keep happening for a long time yet," she agreed.

"What are you doing?"

"Thinking."

"What are you thinking about?"

She sat up, stretched, and looked at me with a hint of a smile on her face. "Shut the door. Can you keep a secret?"

"Sure!" I said, and sat on the edge of the bed.

"Well, I don't know, really," she said. "It was just an idea." She straightened herself, and seemed to be deliberating as to what to tell me. Finally, she said, "How old do you think I look?"

"Huh?"

She scaped her hair back with one hand, and held the other at her neck, framing her face between her arms. "How old do you think I look?"

"I don't know . . . ," I said slowly. "Quite old."

"Older than eleven?"

"Yeah, I suppose so. Yeah."

"That's what I thought, too. I think I look about thirteen, except for this crappy hairstyle and the fact that everyone knows how old I am. You know what I mean. People get so used to you that they don't really *look* at you anymore. Maybe if I looked different, people would treat me differently."

"Like who?" I asked doubtfully. "The people at school?"

"No way. I don't want that lot changing their preconceptions right now."

"Mummy?"

"She doesn't matter. No, I was thinking more of Steven and company. Maybe if I looked a bit older, they wouldn't keep treating me so much like a child." She sighed. "He knows I'm bright, but it's going to be no use at all if he knows I'm a bright *eleven*-year-old."

"He thinks you're twelve," I said.

"Even so. Anyway. People don't talk to kids, so I'd better not be a kid. At least for a while."

"What are you going to do?" I asked, interested.

"Not much. Hang on a bit." She was still wearing the skirt that was a compulsory part of the girls' school uniform, and a plain white blouse. As I sat and watched, she opened her wardrobe and found a pair of jeans. "These'll do. Wait here a while." I blinked as she left the room, and I could hear her go to the bathroom, to the airing cupboard that the hot water tank was in. A few moments later she was back, carrying a white shirt that looked as if it must be my father's. "This is way too big," I heard her mutter.

She shrugged off her skirt and pulled on the jeans instead, and then took off the blouse and substituted the shirt. Its cuffs hung down a good eight inches or so from her wrists, and I started to laugh.

"You look pretty silly," I said.

"Yeah, sure. Wait a bit while I try and sort this out." I waited as she patiently rolled up the sleeves of the shirt until they were bunched casually three-quarters of the way down her forearms. She tucked the loose billows of cloth into the waistband of the jeans. "I could do with a belt," she said.

"I've got one."

"OK, go and get it." I hurried out and returned with the belt.

"Right," Sophie said, as she threaded it through the waistband loops of her jeans. "Close your eyes."

I giggled. "What are you going to do?"

"Never mind. Just shut your eyes, and don't peep or this'll be totally pointless."

"OK," I said, and did so. There was some shuffling, and then the rustle of a plastic bag. I giggled again.

"Shut up," Sophie said, but I could hear the smile in her voice. There was a pause, and then the sound of things being rearranged on her dressing table. Then there was a very long silence, broken suddenly by the hiss of an aerosol spray.

"What are you *doing*?" I said, almost squirming with impatience. "Hurry up. You're taking forever."

"Hang on. I'm nearly done," she said, but there was still an interminable wait before I heard her walk across to stand in front of me.

"Wait," she said. "Don't open your eyes yet. When you do, I want you to try and look at me as if you've never seen me before. Try imagining that it's someone else here, someone you know, and picture them instead of me. When you've got their picture really sharp in your mind, open your eyes quickly. OK?"

"OK," I said.

"Make sure you've got a really good picture of them first," she said.

"OK, OK." I concentrated on imagining one of the girls from my class. At first it was a nebulous attempt, but fairly quickly I managed to get an image of Jacqueline Tynes, who sat in the front row, steady behind my closed eyelids. The room was totally silent; I could hear only my own breathing. When I was almost convinced that it was Jacqueline, and not Sophie, who was standing in front of me, I opened my eyes.

It was a strange shock, but it hit me squarely. I had been concentrating so hard that I had pushed the image of Sophie herself right out of my mind, and when I saw the girl in front of me, two things struck me. The first was that she was not my sister, the second was that she was beautiful.

"How old am I?" Sophie said.

My voice was rough with confusion as I heard myself say, "Fourteen. I think. About that age."

"Good," she said brightly, and the moment she moved away from where she had been standing, that temporary illusion was gone. When I saw her walk, she was suddenly my eleven-year-old sister again.

"You looked really different," I said, struggling to find a way to express what I'd seen. "Have you done something to your hair?"

"Yeah," she said, and pointed to a can of hairspray on the dressing table. "No ponytail, see?"

"Yeah, of course," I said, my voice still sounding odd. She had been astonishingly beautiful, for that single second before she spoke or moved. Now that I was able to notice the details of the change, I found myself more confused than ever. Her hair had been swept forward, so that it fell to the sides of her face rather than at the back in a ponytail; it was held like that with hairspray. And she'd changed her clothes; I'd seen that part.

"Are you wearing makeup?" I said.

"No. Why? Do I look like I am?"

"I don't know," I said. "What else? Other than the clothes and the hair?"

"That's all, really," she said.

"That's it? Just those things?"

"Well," she said, and grinned. "Nearly."

"What is it?" I said. "What else? Come on, tell me!"

"I've been reading books," she said.

"You're always reading books," I said.

"Shut up. And I found out something really interesting—that the way you stand, or sit, or whatever, can change the way people think of you. The way they perceive you. You get it? Before you've even said anything at all, they get an impression of you. And it's a really strong impression, because we all do it without thinking. People interpret it without thinking. But it can be faked."

"Is that what you were doing?" I asked, impressed.

"Yeah. I don't know enough yet, but we'll see. And the hair and stuff is just decoration. It's not so huge a change, after all."

"No," I said. "That's really clever, Sophie." It had occurred to me that this explanation made sense of the transformation in her when she moved. Perhaps she hadn't studied that part of it yet.

"Thanks." She looked at herself in the mirror. "I'd better brush this out before supper."

He stands up, starts to pace the room again. There is tense panic inside me, brought on by the conversation about the barn; there is so much emotion caught up in this—in him—that I am constantly aware that it may break loose. If that happens, I think I am lost. I feel strange; curiously unconcerned one minute, verging on hysteria the next. I can tell that I am exhausted. I think this must be the reason I am unable to keep so tight a hold on myself. I don't know how long we have been here now, but it is several hours. And of course there was the journey here, and everything that happened before that. I need all the reserves of energy I can find.

I am becoming so afraid of this man.

All this is about control. If he has not said that, already, then it has been so strong in what he *has* talked about that I could never have missed it. I can see him, as a child, just beginning to test the relationship for the first time, to dare to push against it, look outside it. But Matthew the child has no control, because Sophie has it all. Which is why I am sitting here now, in this dark room, with candle shadows on the blank walls and the sounds of a dying storm around me.

At the moment, though, it is too simplistic. There will be far more to it, and eventually I will know all the reasons and all the details. I hope.

Thinking of the storm brings it to my attention for the first time in an age. When I concentrate, I find I am right; the sounds are quieter, the rain steady but less heavy, the wind has dropped somewhat. Matthew, still pacing up and down the empty kitchen, gives no indication of being aware of me. These pauses, when he appears to be gathering himself for the next part of his story, must be important to him. It is almost as if, each time, he is working up the courage to continue.

I review everything mentally. I still feel, uncomfortably, that there is something obvious that I am missing. I glance round the room as if I might catch a glimpse of it, whatever it is, in the shadows, but there is nothing.

He turns to me. "How long had you been thinking about it?"

My mind goes blank. "About what?" I ask.

He shakes his head impatiently. "About changing yourself. Re-creating yourself."

I feel a splinter of terror. Carefully, I say, "What are we talking about, Matthew?"

"The hairspray, the clothes. That stuff. You know."

Relief. "Oh. That. I don't know."

"It was very clever. You must have practised at least a little on your own, before showing me. It was—impressive."

I don't know what to say to this.

He goes on, "That was a turning point, I think. Your first glimpse of a different world."

"You mean the adult world?"

"Nearly. That was what you were after, weren't you? I thought about this, afterwards. Thought about it a lot, because it felt important. And do you know something? I really think you were scared. Scared because you couldn't see what was coming next." He exhales, and lets himself sink back to a sitting position across from me. "You'd always lived in a world that was completely known to you. You determined what would happen in it, what would happen *to* it. You even killed off its monsters." He smiles, humourlessly. "And then, on the horizon, you saw changes coming. Small things for everyone else in the world—a new school, being a teenager, things like that. You didn't see them the same way. You saw them as steps away from what you were."

"You're saying I couldn't accept that."

"That's right. You couldn't. I don't know whether you realized right then, but that was it." His face is contorted, almost painful.

I try to move cautiously, hesitantly. "I was afraid?"

"Yes." The word comes out like a sob.

"Did you know?"

He shakes his head again. "Not then. Later. It took me a while to realize what was happening. Sometimes you were—too close to me for me to see you clearly." He takes an uneven breath.

I say, "And what did you feel? When you knew I was afraid?"

His expression twists suddenly to anger. "Oh, for fuck's sake, shut up," he says. "Just stop talking and shut up."

I watch him as he sits. After a time, his breathing settles a little and he raises his head slightly. I wait for him to become calmer, at the same time trying to fight down my own heartbeat, which has sprung up at his unexpected outburst.

We climbed over the wall and cut down into the shadow of the barn, where the morning air still retained its nighttime chill. I went into the barn first, and, sure enough, Andy and Steven were sitting on a bale of straw waiting for us.

"Hi," I said. Sophie stood up just behind me.

"Sorry we're a little late," she said. Her voice was different as well, I noticed. I had kept my eyes on the two boys, though, and it didn't surprise me at all to see them both straighten a little where they were sitting, as if to get a better look at Sophie. She went on, "It's our half-term now, so there's lots we can do. Come on up." She started up the little steps to the open room of the fort.

"Lots to do like what?" Steven said, following her.

"That's what I want to talk about."

"You still sound like a fucking teacher," he said.

"Yeah." She sounded bored. I found a corner to sit in and got out my planes, arranging them in my lap. The other three had moved slightly together, as if in conference. I let my eyes drop, and pretended not to be listening to them.

"So?" Steven was saying. "What sort of things?"

"I don't know. I thought you could suggest some," Sophie replied. "You know. Something a little interesting. After all, you've got this place now, out of sight and out of mind, as they say. If you want to play houses in it, then that's fine, but I imagined you could think up some better ideas."

"Playing houses is about all you've done," he said, looking around.

"Looks that way, doesn't it? So if anyone *does* come across this lot, they'll assume it's just some kids playing. That's pretty normal. That's what you thought when you first found it, isn't it?"

"Yeah," he agreed reluctantly. "OK, then. Sophie here wants to do something different." He looked at Andy and grinned. I moved the fighter planes in my lap mechanically, and kept listening. "Grown-up things, you mean?" The sarcasm in his voice was very obvious.

"If you know any," Sophie said.

Steven laughed. "Yeah, just none that you're capable of. I mean, what do you want to do? Get pissed and tell rude jokes? Read dirty books? Smoke dope? Christ."

Sophie looked up with interest. "Can you get hold of drugs?" she said. Steven's jaw dropped, and for a moment he just sat there looking comically surprised.

"What the fuck are you talking about?"

"You said did I want to smoke dope. That's drugs, isn't it? I want to know if you can get hold of any."

Steven shook his head, half admiringly. "You are so funny," he said, absently. "I can't believe I'm sitting here listening to this. You can't do dope at your age, for fuck's sake."

"Why not?" Sophie asked.

"Jesus! You're only *twelve*, don't you understand? Besides, you couldn't afford it on your pocket-money."

"Money," Sophie said, slowly. "OK, I see. But there's not any biological reason why not, is there?"

"Probably. Maybe it blows your head off if you don't have pubes yet. It's just something you're going to have to wait a few years for, that's all." He grinned and sat back.

"Have you done it?" Sophie asked.

"Sure, of course I have. There's a guy I know who gets hold of gear at school, if anyone wants any."

"So you could get some, then?" she continued.

Steven shook his head again. "You just don't give up, do you?" he said.

"If you're sure you can get some," Sophie said, "we could talk about money now."

Across from me, Sophie and Steven eyed each other thoughtfully. Nothing much more was said for a while, and after a time Sophie seemed content to let the conversation stray back to more ordinary topics, as if her comment about money had been a joke. I thought that Steven had probably realized that she meant it, though, and was just messing around, trying to make up his own mind. For my own part, I was surprised at what Sophie had been saying, but not shocked; I had almost imagined that she would be interested in something like this. It was the next stage, and I recognized that; she was looking to extend herself, to stretch out a small way towards the world of adulthood, to become involved in the possibilities of adolescence. I could see easily enough that she thought it was about time; she was obviously impatient with childhood.

"Sophie?"

She looked up. "Yes, Mattie? What is it?"

"I'm bored," I said. "Can I go and play?"

"Yeah," she said. "Stick around, though. You can go up to the woods and so on. You got a watch?"

"Yes."

"Then don't be gone more than a couple of hours."

I could tell from her voice that she was half pleased. I scrambled down from the straw, ran across the barn and ducked out into the sunlight.

•   •   •

"You didn't really need me there," he says. He doesn't sound re-sentful; he is merely stating a fact. I allow myself to nod agree-ment. He continues, "I understood that better than you think. I knew what you were doing, and I didn't mind. I thought—if she does this now, this finding out, then she'll always come back later."

"You thought that?"

"Why not? Does it sound unusual?"

"For a nine-year-old, yes, it does."

He shrugs. "Maybe. I learnt a lot from you, remember. I could see you so easily vanishing into all the new worlds you'd find when you left home."

"Left you, you mean."

"If you like." He stares at the floor, apparently thinking. After the sudden flare of temper a while ago, he is cool now, cautious. I wonder if he thinks I have been provoking him deliberately. He'd be wrong to think that, of course; that will come later, if at all. It's too big a risk to play around with. For the moment, he seems withdrawn. I shift my balance a little, trying to relieve the pressure on my back.

He says, "I think you underestimated me a lot."

That is certainly true. I tell him, "Maybe I did."

# eleven

When I got back to the farm, I was surprised to see, from the lane, a figure standing in the courtyard. As I got closer, I quickly identified it as Andy, and as I watched, he wandered into the open-fronted shed where Sophie and I had found the iron bar with which to break into the barn. Intrigued, I followed him, instead of going straight to see Sophie, and when I caught up with him he was sitting on a workbench at the end of the shed, swinging his feet and whistling quietly.

"Oh!" he exclaimed, when he saw me, and then, "Hi. You gave me a fright."

"Where are the others?" I asked.

"Still talking. Steve said I should go for a walk." I sat down on one of the oil drums. Andy had light brown hair, and freckles across his nose. He didn't fit my hazy memory of bullying at school, but then that had been—four years ago, I worked out. "Your sister's something else."

"What do you mean?"

He shrugged. "You know. She's really strange. She must be bloody clever."

"She is, I think," I said. I was cautious, but it didn't feel as if there was any guile in Andy's comments. If anything, he sounded puzzled, and a bit scared.

"What do you think she wants?" he asked.

"I don't know. I don't understand it," I said. "Maybe she just wants to find things out."

Andy looked at me steadily. "I can believe that," he said. "She's pretty cool about it all. Like she's halfway between a headmistress and Jesus Christ. I can't *believe* the way she just said to Steve, 'Let's do drugs,' or whatever it was. It was fucking unreal."

I grinned. "I thought it was funny," I said. "Did you see what his face looked like?"

"I'll say," Andy said. "Looked like someone hit him with a dead fish." For some reason, I found this wildly appropriate, and snorted with laughter.

"She's sometimes a bit—surprising," I said, when I'd got my breath back.

"It must be pretty rough," Andy said. "Living with her, I mean."

"Not really," I said. The comment was unexpected. "She's OK, really. She just doesn't . . . get on with people too well. Other people. You know what I mean."

"Doesn't make friends easily?"

"I don't think so. Not real friends. School friends, yeah, but not generally. I mean, *everyone* has school friends."

"You got any proper friends, then?" he asked.

I thought about it. "I don't know. Sophie, of course."

"Must be odd, liking your sister," he said. "Steve and I can't stand each other most of the time."

"Yeah," I said. I didn't know what else to say.

Andy stretched, and then got down from the workbench. "Shall we see what's going on?" he said.

"OK." We went back into the barn. Steven was smoking a cigarette, looking uncomfortable, while Sophie was sitting cross-legged, smiling slightly.

"Hi," she said. "Enjoy yourself?"

"Yeah," I said. "What have you been doing?"

"Deciding things," Sophie said, and then uncrossed her legs and stood up. Again, I was caught off guard by the way she looked; she seemed to be half someone else, someone I hadn't seen before. "I reckon we've had enough. See you guys on Wednesday, then."

"Yeah," Steven said. He was looking slightly nervous. "Look, if I get caught, what am I going to say?"

"Just say it's for you," Sophie said. "You're only fifteen. Nobody's going to give a fuck."

He blinked. "Right, OK," he muttered. Sophie smiled brightly.

"Come on, Mattie," she said. "Let's go home."

The days until Wednesday passed with a strange kind of excited tension in the air. Sophie wandered aimlessly about the house a lot of the time until, early on Monday afternoon, she headed off to the quarry with me in tow, walking quickly and eagerly. We spent nearly three hours there, Sophie scribbling away for long periods of time and then pausing to stare thoughtfully at the sky or the ground, chewing the end of her Biro, her face frowning with concentration. I managed a few more cursory glances at the quarry books, but their ordered columns of nonsense words were nothing I hadn't seen before, and I soon grew bored. I made a series of forays into the woods surrounding the quarry, doubling back every now and again to let Sophie know where I was. At night, I could hear her moving around her room long after she was normally in bed.

Wednesday, when it arrived, was a disappointment. Sophie

and Steven sat and talked in the straw fort for a while, until eventually Sophie suggested that Andy and I go for a walk or something for a couple of hours. Quite able to recognize a hint, I thought about protesting, but then decided that it would probably not be worth the effort. Instead, I followed Andy out into the brittle daylight and we strolled around the farmyard for a time.

I said, "We could go down by the stream and look for sticklebacks."

"I don't know," he said. I thought he looked uneasy.

"What do you think they're doing?" I asked.

"Not much. Probably just smoking stuff. I bet your sister's sick," he added. "I was, first time I tried smoking."

"Were you?" I said, impressed. "I don't think I've ever seen Sophie sick." We sat down on the steps of one of the buildings, looking out towards the village.

"Doesn't she get ill, then?" Andy asked, half amused.

"Not really. I can't remember her being ill. Except when— oh," I said.

"What?"

"Except that time at school," I said, embarrassed.

"Which was that?" he said.

"You know. The one with—with the other boy, and you." I knew well enough that I wasn't making much sense, but Andy understood me. I watched, scared, as a shadow of emotion passed through his face; for a second, he looked genuinely angry, and I was afraid.

Then, surprisingly calmly, he said, "You know that wasn't me, don't you?"

"I—"

The memory of that day had faded, so much so that I couldn't recall the faces or names of the two boys involved—

only that there had been two, and that Sophie had been badly hurt. But sitting there on the steps in the thin autumn sunlight, I thought that, inside my head, I could suddenly see our headmaster's study, and Sophie sitting on a chair, and people in the room. There was a bruise on her cheek, and my eyes focused mainly on that, and on the adults. But I clearly remembered her eyes, and, looking at them now across however many years, I could recognize that they were not hurt, or afraid. Maybe I'd even known that at the time.

Andy said, "She did that to herself."

"I know," I said.

"Yeah. Thought you probably did." He stood up, shoved his hands into his jeans pockets, and took a few steps out across the cobbles. He was looking across to the other side of the road, where the gentle curve of the hill opposite our house rose towards the village. He stood like that for a long time, while I plundered the fragment of memory for all I was worth, trying to root from it things that I didn't want to know.

"I'm sorry," I said at last.

I didn't think he was going to answer. "Yeah," he said at last. "It wasn't your fault, though. I mean, there wasn't anything you could do. I know I deserved—" He stopped, and then said, almost in a whisper, "We were just kids. Nobody meant any harm." He seemed to be thinking, until he turned around and squatted down facing me. His expression was easier, more open, and I felt myself relax. "Do you like Sophie?"

"Yeah."

"You love her?"

"Yeah, I suppose so," I said, uncomfortably.

"Christ." He shook his head. "She's not normal, Mattie. You know that?"

"I—I don't know," I said, and I think the intensity of his voice must have sparked something inside me, because I found myself on the edge of tears.

When Andy saw that, he stopped, and swallowed. "It's OK," he said. "Just make sure you don't get hurt. You don't want to get in her way."

"Mmm."

I sat looking at my shoes until he pushed my arm gently. "Hey, don't look so sad. If it makes any difference, she seems to give a fuck about you. Must be an odd feeling, having her around all the time." He grinned. "Like having your personal nuclear bomb with you, twenty-four hours a day."

I smiled, rather tearfully.

"What about we go and do something else? They're going to be in there for another hour and a half, easily."

"Yeah," I said. "Smoking and being sick."

"Smoking and puking, right," he agreed. "So. What d'you want to do?"

I got to my feet. "I'm going to show you the woods, up there," I said, pointing.

"Sounds good to me."

Sophie was quieter than usual when we walked home. That evening, when I had got ready for bed and brushed my teeth, I went through to her room. She was sitting on her bed with her knees drawn up, staring thoughtfully at the ceiling.

"Hi," she said.

"Hi. What happened?"

"At the barn?" She raised her eyebrows, and I nodded. "Come and sit down, then," she added. I knelt by the side of the bed and folded my arms on it, looking at her.

"Not a lot, basically. We smoked some stuff that Steven brought. What are you laughing about?"

"Were you sick?" I asked.

"No. Why, did you think I would be?"

"I don't know," I said. "Maybe."

Sophie smiled, and then laughed. "Yeah, it wasn't very nice to start with."

"What was it like?"

She shrugged. "Not a lot, like I said. You feel quite calm, it's quite pleasant. After you get used to the smoking part. That's pretty odd. But other than that, you just feel kind of sleepy but without wanting to go to sleep."

"Oh," I said. "That's all?"

"Yeah."

"If that's one drug, are others different?" I asked.

"I don't know," Sophie said. "Maybe they feel different, but maybe it's just the same effect, only stronger."

"Are you going to find out?"

She scratched her ear. "Probably not," she said. "Steve's practically shitting himself just because we did this. I don't think he'd get hold of anything else. But at least I tried it." She was looking less pensive and more pleased with herself, now.

"Four more days to go," I said. Sophie blinked, and then nodded.

"Right. Didn't know what you were talking about for a second. What do you want to do with your four more days of freedom, then?"

"I've got a project to do," I said reluctantly.

"Yeah. Well, if you get that done tomorrow, we'll do something different on Friday. I've got to go into the village in any case, so you won't be missing anything."

"OK," I said. "I've done my teeth."

"Off you go, then," she said. "See you tomorrow."

"And you," I said, and closed her bedroom door behind me. Downstairs, I could hear my mother walking round the drawing room, her feet slow and muted on the deep carpet. Every now and again a board creaked. I shut my door tightly, and climbed into bed. On the floor near the window was the textbook and the sheets of paper for the project. Sophie had said she was going into the village tomorrow, which meant she'd probably be going to the library, and would probably be gone most of the morning. I turned the thought around in my head, and looked at the clock on my bedside table. It was five past nine. I didn't feel too tired, I told myself. I could stay awake quite a long time, if I wanted to.

There was a pen with the paper. I gathered it all up, brought it back to the bed with me, and settled down with the book propped up on my knees as a support. Then I stopped, looking at the line of light from the hallway under the door. I got up again, took my dressing gown down from its peg, and laid it across the bottom of the door. Once I'd arranged everything again on the covers of my bed, I took the first sheet of paper and wrote carefully, *Leonardo da Vinci. By Matthew Howard.* I looked at the clock; it was eight minutes past, now. I grinned to myself and continued writing.

"I think it was the first time I consciously set about deceiving you," he says. "Sometimes I can't believe I ever did it. And other times, I look at it and I can't believe I hadn't done it before."

"Never before?" I ask.

"I don't think so. Not like this—deliberately. I worked it out ahead of time, planned it. That was what you did. I wasn't used to thinking that way, to begin with."

"Why not?"

"Because you'd always been there to do it for me," he says shortly. "The funny thing was, once I'd been at it for a while, it became easy. As if that part of me had been there all along, and only needed a little push to get going." He looks at me, straight. "It was frightening, but I liked it."

"What did you like?" I ask, trying to keep him talking about this.

"The feeling of exhilaration. Knowing that I could trick you."

I can't help asking it. "It was that important to you?"

"Damn it, Sophie! Of course it was! What did you think was going on?" He shakes his head. "Sometimes I used to think that, without you, I'd be nothing at all. That I'd just vanish. I could never even *imagine* a life without you. It was as if I had to draw on you for everything." He runs out of breath and stops, looking dazed. There is a long pause. Eventually, his voice much quieter, he says, "I hardly realized this. Not in words. But the feeling was there constantly, you know? I couldn't escape it. It was always there."

He lapses into silence once again. I wait patiently for him to continue.

Sophie left soon after breakfast. I hung around the house for longer, taking my time; my mother was nowhere to be seen yet. Sophie had taken a plastic carrier bag with her, and was wearing what I had started to think of as her "new" clothes, the ones that made her look older. In fact, it was hard sometimes not to think of her as a "new" Sophie, since each day she became more at home with the persona she had adopted, and made it work for her better. So thinking, I pulled on my trainers, trying not to yawn. I had forgotten at what time I got to sleep the night before, but there were six or so completed sheets of project on the floor beside the bed, which was more than reasonable for a morning's work, if Sophie chose to look at it. No, I corrected myself; the choice shouldn't be left up to her. I would make sure that she saw what I had been doing, so that she would know I had been stuck in the house all morning. I brushed my teeth, without much conviction, and stared out of the window, and had some more squash, until a full twenty minutes had passed by the clock on the kitchen wall. Even then, I peered around the side of the house carefully, making sure the lane was free, before I started off across the garden and up the hill.

I walked swiftly, setting my feet on the rocky outcroppings that marked where the path had been eroded. Hunks of brown vegetation had slumped in the shadow of the wall, testimony to the death of summer, and there were beadings of moisture on the nettle leaves and on the stones in the path. The laces of my trainers were soon soaked through with dew from the coarse grass that overhung the edges of the path. There was a thin, steady, early-morning breeze, and the sun, where it had come up over the tree line to my left, was pale.

I reached the outskirts of the wood that surrounded the quarry and paused for a minute, crouched down by the wall. I was wearing the dark blue anorak that I didn't normally wear; it was getting too small, and I had a much nicer one now. But the colour was sombre and wouldn't, I thought, show up clearly from a distance. I knew that I was in all probability making too much of a fuss, but where Sophie was concerned this seemed less like paranoia and more like common sense. There was a keen, sharp excitement in my chest, as if the cold air had frozen something in there. When I had got my breath back somewhat, I crunched through the frayed rim of bracken that marked the boundary between field and trees, and stepped into the wood. There was a sudden crash and scurry, across to my right, and my heart leapt inside me for a second. Some wild animal, I told my-self, and started on again. The birds overhead were circling and calling.

The shale and loose rock at the lip of the quarry, and on the path down, were wet with dew or with night rain; I wasn't sure which. I set my feet carefully, one after the other, and sideways on so as to maintain a better grip on the incline, just as Sophie had shown me. With one arm half outstretched behind me for balance, I made my way without incident to the bottom of the quarry, and looked around. The sky overhead was the colour of old metal gone white, and at one point I saw two or three dark birds wander lazily into my field of vision, and then move away again into the world beyond the quarry. There was a strange, alien sensation in me, and for several minutes I couldn't work out what it was. And then I realized that I had never been in the quarry alone; never been here, not even once before, without Sophie beside me.

I shivered, and set off less determinedly across the quarry floor. Scattered around were rocks that I recognized, especially the ones too big to move, which had sat there, unchanged and unchanging, ever since I had first seen this place. That would have been four—no, five years ago. Over there was where Sophie normally sat to write; over there, the place where we had once had a picnic; over there, the place I had found my best fossil, the one I had given to Sophie. The days of the fossils and the rock hammer seemed so very far away, measured against their memory. The air seemed colder down here, and I rubbed my arms vigorously. I found that I had come right across the quarry floor to the start of the slope that led to the cages.

I looked up at their blank openings and swallowed uncomfortably. Sophie had told me about them; abandoned workings that had been closed off with bars to stop people playing in them. It seemed a waste, to me; I couldn't imagine anyone wanting to go inside one of the cages, for whatever reason. Especially, for some reason, the farthest one, into which I had once—many years ago—thrown a rock. The cage had swallowed that up, and

I knew in my belly that it would swallow me up, too, if I were able to go inside. Even the smell of them was disquieting; it seeped between the bars to dissipate in the fresher air outside, but if you were close enough you could smell it. At the foot of the farthest cage, held down by a rock and protected in part by an overhang in the quarry wall, was the canvas bag. I retrieved it, and then stood, suddenly more scared than I had been, and not knowing what to do. If I went back to the centre of the quarry, I was in full view. But if I stayed here, I was only three feet or so from the cage. For a long moment I hesitated, my mind whirling, and then I trotted hastily down again to the open arena of the quarry floor. I didn't think that Sophie would come. She had gone into town. . . . In the back of my mind, I wondered what she would do if she *did* find me here.

I took the biscuit tin out of the bag and put it down in front of me. It was a large, square tin, and the legends round the sides proclaimed that it had once held a teatime assortment. Much of the red paint had been battered and flaked off, through constant friction with the other contents of the bag; the screwdriver, chisels, hammer, were all there, as if I could step back into the past if I felt like it, and pick them up once again. I studied the tin carefully, noting where scratches continued across from its body to its lid. I squared it in front of me, and then prised the lid off and set it beside the tin, keeping its alignment identical. I had no idea whether Sophie would have marked the tin in some way, or whether she simply relied on the location of the quarry to guard it for her, but I was reluctant to take any chances at all.

Inside, there were several plastic bags, their openings twisted round and secured with clothes pegs. Inside were the rather tattered exercise books in which Sophie kept her sort-of diary. I undid one carefully and opened the book inside. Line after line and page after page was filled with jumbled idiocy. It was one of the earlier books; there were none of the neat columns of letters I had seen in her more recent writings. There seemed to be no dates, no obvious breaks from one section to the next, except an occasional change in the ink colour of the Biro she had used. I looked through it carefully, and then flicked back to the beginning. From my pocket, I took the paper and pen I had brought with me, and laboriously started to copy out the first page of the quarry book.

For the first time, I interrupt him. "What made you choose the quarry books?" I say. "I thought you were scared of them."

He looks up, startled. "Why did I choose them? Because they were the biggest secret, I suppose."

"Is that true?"

He looks at me, and there is something strange almost hidden in his eyes. "Is what true?"

"That they were the biggest secret."

He laughs. "At that point, they were," he says, and laughs again. I feel myself shiver, and the candle flame—burnt low now—flickers and darts in the centre of the floor.

I pulled shut the door of my bedroom after taking a quick look around the house and satisfying myself that Sophie was not back yet. It was just past midday, and there was an hour or so before lunchtime. I knew perfectly well that I was unlikely to see my mother if I was careful, and that she would assume Sophie had taken care of me. I didn't know when Sophie was planning to return, but I felt confident that I would hear her when she did.

Sitting on the floor by my bed, I spread out the pages of my Leonardo project in a convincingly chaotic fashion, and then took from my pocket the four folded sheets of paper onto which

I had transcribed passages of the quarry books. I had taken one segment—the first page, in each case—from each of the four books in the biscuit tin. They had been the thick blue exercise books that had been phased out at our school about a year before and replaced with thinner types with a variety of brightly coloured covers. I started with the one I had assumed was the earliest; there was a degree of change in Sophie's handwriting over the course of the sequence, and I had been able to assign the passages a chronological order fairly easily.

I stared at the meaningless strings of letters in incomprehension for five minutes before shaking my head and deciding to try a more organized approach. The first thing I tried was reading the passage backwards, but that made no sense at all. I tried writing out the alphabet on another sheet, and seeing whether that helped. I tried substituting one letter for another, but my own ignorance of the best ways to do this left me confused and irritable. By one o'clock, I had had enough; I folded the four sheets carefully, and then stopped, trying to decide what to do with them. If I hid them, there was no guarantee that Sophie would not find them. She knew everywhere I went, everything I did. The only secret place that I had was inside my own head.

I took the papers out into the garden, down behind one of the sheds in the orchard, and burned them.

# twelve

**H**e is not telling me everything. I have been sure of that for some time now. I think everything he has said has been the truth, but he is avoiding something that is central to it all. If I knew him better, perhaps I could judge what it is that he is withholding; but one of the things that has been brought home to me in the course of this night is that I know Matthew hardly at all.

There is another side to that, of course. He doesn't know me, either. He is seeing me as an echo of his childhood—but that childhood only exists in his head.

The storm has subsided. The rain hisses and patters outside, but there is no more lightning, and the wind has fallen. Matthew doesn't appear to have noticed. He sits, head down, as if buried deep in thought. It occurs to me to wonder how he sees this from his point of view—whether it all makes perfect sense, or whether he is aware of the discontinuities, the lesions between his story and the real world of this room. In a strange way, I think he is beginning to be. He seems not as sure of himself as before, and the pauses when he stops talking and waits in silence have become more frequent. At times, he looks like a man struggling.

I watch him, seeing this, and am scared; I don't know what the struggle is about, or what I might precipitate by interfering.

It might be my imagination, but I think I can see a faint lightening of the darkness glimpsed between the boards of the window.

At the weekends, more often than not, Sophie and I would meet up with Steven and Andy at the barn. Sometimes we would all stay there, talking, but generally Andy and I left the other two alone and went off to other parts of the farm, or to the woods on the hill above. I found, rather to my surprise, that I liked Andy, and enjoyed being with him. We talked about most things, and he told me about the school he was at, which sounded very different from anything I had experienced. I told him that Sophie might be going to a boarding school—something she'd only recently mentioned to me—and he laughed, and said that was fine if you could afford it. He also said that it might be the best place for her, which I found funny but also disturbing, because it made me think of having to live at home for two years without Sophie.

We left crisp tracks in early morning frosts on these walks, and our breath trailed away behind us ethereally before fading into transparency. When we talked about sex, I was surprised and pleased to find that I knew more, in a technical sense, than Andy did, although he knew about things the books didn't mention. We traded jokes, and I told him about asthma, and we decided that we were a splinter group from the barn. The sun and sky had turned to winter by now, and Christmas was within sight.

On the last day of school, Sophie was waiting for me by the gate, surrounded by struggling children clasping paintings and costumes for the end of term show, along with school books and satchels stuffed with belongings. By contrast, she was carrying just a shoulder bag, although I was laden with stuff.

"Hi," she said. "Do you want me to carry some of that? Look, if I take this big thing here, you can use both hands for the rest of it."

"All right," I said quickly, and let her take a long cardboard tube filled with rolled-up pictures.

"We're hardly early at all," she said, disapprovingly. "Never mind. What do you say we get a can of something and some sweets before we go home?"

"Yeah, sure! Why?"

"I don't know. It's the end of term. We should celebrate." We went left instead of right out of the gates, and made slow progress as far as the high street, where Sophie ducked into a shop and bought food and drink. Returning with her pockets bulging, she said, "Right. Head for home." I nodded, and we set off.

Christmas itself was usually a dull time at our house. This year it was both better and worse; my father remained away, wherever he was, and the time I spent actually inside the house was for the most part intolerably boring. Of course, all this meant in practice was that Sophie and I took every opportunity to escape, despite the weather. My mother never made any protest, or, if she did, I never heard it. By this time, Sophie was running the house, and although no one would ever have said such a thing, I think my mother and I both knew it to be true.

We would head out at dawn and spend our time at any of our several places, depending mostly on the weather. I could sit and read quietly in the seclusion of the holly bush for a morning, or, if the rain was heavy, we could run across the fields to the barn and stay there for the day. We would talk, and I would play with my fighters or draw pictures, and Sophie would sit reading or thinking. As the holiday progressed, I noticed that she spent more and more time absorbed in her own thoughts. We bought new batteries for the torches in our concealed room, and new candles for the holly bush.

Secretly, we were both planning the presents we would give the other for Christmas, and Sophie told me she had decided to hold a Christmas party in the straw fort, so we were collaborating to decorate it with holly and other greenery. It was an exciting time, and we enjoyed it together.

"Come on," Sophie said. "What have you lost?"

"My anorak."

"It's in the hall where you left it."

Suitably clothed, we set off for the quarry. The sky was clear but covered by a thin mist of winter cloud, high up, so that it looked like frosted glass. The white sun was still low over the trees as we climbed the hill.

"Are we going to see Andy and Steven soon?" I asked.

"Maybe. I haven't really thought," Sophie said casually. I knew it wasn't true; she had always thought things out beforehand. "There's a new hairdresser opened in town."

"Yeah?"

"Yeah. I thought I might go there and see what difference it makes."

"You're getting vain," I told her.

"So? Girls are allowed to be vain. It's part of our personality profile. We can get away with lots of things boys can't."

"Oh." There didn't seem to be much else to say.

"And I should buy some clothes as well," she went on. "But carefully. I don't want people noticing. Shop assistants get worried if kids spend money."

"What are you going to buy?"

"Some jeans. Decent ones. And some tops. You know, sort of sweatshirt things. And I'm going to get a bra."

"Really?"

"Yeah. I don't really need one all that much, but what the fuck. I'll get one of those tiny little things for nervous teenagers."

We got to the edge of the quarry and began to work our way down. I was struck suddenly by the thought that this was the first time we had visited the quarry since I had come here alone. What if I had made a mistake, and Sophie noticed something was wrong? I could feel my heart hammering faster, and the air seemed to have turned very dry.

"—in any case. Yeah?"

"What?" I said.

"Wake up. I said I look thirteen in any case."

"Yeah, you probably do," I said.

"We won't stay too long. There's lots else to do, and it's pretty cold."

"OK. I'll get the bag, if you like."

"Fair enough." We walked together to the middle of the quarry, and then I went up to the cages and retrieved the bag. As I walked back to where Sophie was standing, I felt as if I were carrying a grenade in my hands. I passed it to her.

"Thanks." She opened the tin, unwrapped the latest book, and turned to a new page. Unconsciously, I had been holding my breath, but at this I let it out, and it formed a drifting haze in front of my face.

"I'm going to look round the woods," I said.

"I'll be about ten minutes," she replied. "Don't go too far. Watch out for bears and stuff."

"Bears hibernate in winter," I said, feeling pleased with myself, and Sophie laughed.

"So they do. Now piss off, you're spoiling my concentration."

I grinned, and made off back the way we had come, relief flooding through me that I had not been discovered. At the top of the incline I looked back down at Sophie, sitting on a rock, a small colourful figure hunched over the book she was resting on her knees.

Later that afternoon, we talked about the Christmas party.

"We'll have it in the upper room," she said. "A proper secret party."

"Who else will be there?"

"No one but us." She thought for a second. "And I think we should have it at midnight."

"Yeah? Really?"

"Why not? It would be pretty cool. We'll get some food and stuff. And bring the torches up. We can cover them with some of that crêpe paper, make them different colours."

I was immediately enthusiastic. "Yeah! That would be really great. When do we get it ready?"

"This weekend. It had better be fairly soon. Christmas is—a week on Thursday. It's not long."

"I've never had a real party before," I said.

"Yeah, I know. Well, this is the last Christmas before—you know, before I go away. So I thought we'd make it special."

"Oh." When she said that, I felt suddenly cold.

We were at the top of the rise now, and could see down into the next dip in the landscape. Off in one direction I could see the roofs of the town, and the snaking roads leading out away from it. Back the way we had come, our house was out of sight around the shoulder of the hill. Sophie was carrying our lunch in a plastic bag.

"There's so much to be done," she went on. "Exciting, isn't it?"

"It is," I said. I wished she hadn't reminded me about next year, and new schools, and her going away.

"Let's go down there. We can sit on the wall and eat, if you like."

"OK. I'm getting hungry," I said.

"Race you." She was off and running before I realized what she had said.

"That's not *fair!*"

• • •

He stays silent for a moment, rubbing his face with one hand as if trying to decide something. When he speaks, it is almost in a whisper.

"I've never got this far before," he says.

Instinctively, I know what he means. "In the story?"

He nods. "Yeah. I—when I tried before, I could never get far enough."

His face is twisted, as if in pain. "Wait a bit," I say, surprised at myself for my calmness. I have no idea whether this development is to my advantage or not.

With a sudden, unpleasant jolt of recognition, I realize that I am behaving exactly as he has accused me—secretively, hiding things, inspecting opportunities that I may be able to use. I find I am shocked by the thought that I can be, even in part, the way he sees me.

He says, "The real problem was that I didn't realize—until afterwards—how much I loved you. It took absence to force that on me. You filled up my whole world. You were my barrier against the outside."

"Was it just love?"

Immediately, I wonder if I have made a mistake. The last thing I need to do now is to anger him, make him lose this tenuous link to whatever constitutes the rest of his story.

To my relief, he appears to consider the question seriously. "Back then? I think so." He hesitates, then continues. "Perhaps not afterwards."

"After—I went away?"

"After you went away," he agrees gravely.

"How did you feel after that?"

He shakes his head, almost irritably. "I don't know. Confused. Angry. Scared."

"OK, OK," I say. He stops, looks at me, and then slumps a little where he sits.

"Let's get it over with," he says.

Next summer, Sophie was twelve and I was ten. Over that year, few things changed in our town: the buildings of the farm showed the marks of the past winter in fallen slates and loosened window boards, but otherwise the time hardly showed. The quarry was as immutable as ever, while the landscape that surrounded us adapted from season to season without hesitation. Between the two of us, however, there were some changes. Sophie was growing up; it was suddenly evident that she stood noticeably taller than me, where before the difference was marginal. Her face had altered subtly, a change large enough for me to have noticed but at the same time not large enough to be easily described. Her manner of speech had altered as well, and she was more likely to use in the company of adults or other children those same speech patterns that she had used with me, in private, for years. She became suddenly more conscientious about locking the bathroom door after her. Some of these changes I found amusing, and some exasperating, but as a whole they worried me secretly. I saw them as evidence that Sophie was getting ready to move on, make a break from childhood. I was afraid of being left behind.

It didn't work out quite like that, though. In Sophie's final year at our school, the subject of exams came up once again. It was decided that Sophie should try for an academic scholarship to a private school some fifty miles away. I remember the visit we made to look at the school, which left me with an impression of great scale, with many buildings and many pupils. And without the uniform to distinguish them, the pupils would have been women; they looked far too old to be still at school. Sophie

looked about her with evident interest, and I could see her mentally filing her observations for scrutiny later. She was quiet most
of the time we were being shown around; her eyes were busy,
picking out people and classrooms and teachers as if photograph-
ing them. She was quiet on the way home, too, but I thought I
could sense that she was feeling positive. She sat in the back of the
car with her arms folded, looking thoughtful but comfortable, as
if she had had confirmation of her preconceptions.

When the time came for the exam, she worked for it very seriously, very carefully. She noted down the different subjects she
would have to take papers in, and set aside an hour or so of each
evening for revision. Once in a while she would spend this hour
in the kitchen, with her books and notes spread out on the larger
table there, as if she was reminding my mother and me that she
was working hard. And it was at about this time that I came
across the eight or so *Test Your Own IQ* paperbacks, with their
scores filled in and tabulated. Sophie didn't talk much to me
about the exam, as if she was determined to face this goal alone.
For my part, I was quite content to let her: I didn't understand
the schoolwork she was revising, and knew that I would have
found it boring if I had. But more than this, I was convinced—
although I said nothing—that Sophie's intentions were different
to the expectations of her teachers, and that something was going to happen to surprise them. Secretly, I hoped that she was
planning to fail her exams, so that she wouldn't be able to go
away. The concept was nebulous in my mind, and I failed to examine it closely, but I was sure that Sophie was capable of engi-
neering things so that she wouldn't have to move to a school
that was, to my mind, so distant.

With the same precision by which she guaranteed herself
an IQ of 125, Sophie failed the scholarship exam. She must
have been among the highest-scoring of the "failures," however,

because the school offered her a place without the need to take any further tests. Apart from some confused disappointment among her teachers, there was no real fuss made. Perhaps they had overestimated her somewhat. Perhaps she had just had a bad day. Sophie, smiling slightly, remained quiet, although she, too, was just disappointed enough to make people sympathetic. She was bright, but not quite *that* bright. And the one or two teachers who had maybe noticed anomalies in Sophie's progress over the years—occasional flashes of brilliance, remarks that were precociously incisive for a child of her age—were reassured by this yardstick of her actual ability.

I knew well enough that her score in the exam had been deliberate, and I asked her about it.

"I don't want to be too conspicuous; it doesn't do. Besides, I got in, didn't I? It's only crummy prestige they were aiming for in any case. We don't *need* a scholarship."

"I s'pose so," I said. "Do you think you'll enjoy it?"

"Probably." She sounded distant.

"Will you come home at the weekends?"

She laughed. "Don't worry, I'm not deserting you. You'll be OK. You will, won't you? Not going to get lonely on me?"

"I'll try not to," I said.

"Good. 'Cos that wouldn't do, either." She sounded confident, and there was a strength in her voice that I hadn't really noticed before—or at least, not to this degree.

"Right," I said, and felt a bit better.

"And we've still got the summer," she added. "Lots of time there. It's not really a good-bye, after all."

It was difficult to see in those terms. I looked forward to the summer as a time of ending; and when I look back, it still feels the same way.

The end of the school year hit us with an end of term show,

presented outside and at the mercy of the weather, was a great success. The evening was fine, and the parents took their places on the rows of plastic seats while the action unfolded on a stage set up against the outside wall of the assembly hall. We both had parts—I as a spear-bearing soldier, Sophie as a lady. She had some lines, and delivered them clearly and with a touch of humour that lifted the scene she was in. At the end of the play, when the cast came together for a final scene in front of the cardboard battlements of the castle, the applause was loud and we were all tired. We cleaned off our makeup in the school bathrooms and waited for our mother to drive us home.

The last day was as mindlessly chaotic as usual. I met Sophie in the corridor, both of us hurrying on separate errands, and she smiled and raised her eyebrows at me.

"Everyone's running around like chickens," she said. "Half my class is hysterical. All the girls are crying."

"Yeah," I agreed. "It's always like that."

When the doors opened at four o'clock, the sudden exodus flooded the playground and the road outside until it was hardly possible to leave the school if you were in a car. Sophie surveyed the scene from the main steps.

"We'd do better going out the side gate," she said. "Come on."

It was a longer route, normally, but we avoided the crush and made it to our road without being stopped by anyone. The day was warm, and there was the anticipation of summer everywhere. I kicked a stone along the tarmac in front of me as we walked.

"Do you feel nervous?"

"No. It's going to be fine. Let's not talk about it, hey? We'll just have a bloody good time for a couple of months. OK?"

"OK," I said, and smiled. "That sounds good."

Several things happened that summer, the summer before Sophie went away. The first part of the holiday was quiet; there was nothing to hint at what was to come. We both had our birthdays, and I was amused by the thought of Sophie being a teenager.

"What's it feel like, being thirteen?"

"Same as being twelve," she said. "Not any different. What's it feel like being eleven?"

I grinned. "It's OK."

"I'm going down to town this afternoon. You want to come with me?"

"Where are you going?"

"Just shopping and other stuff. Maybe buy some clothes."

"You have a uniform," I pointed out.

She looked blank for a moment. "Oh. That's for next year," she said. "I meant for now."

"I think I'll stay here," I said.

"Suit yourself. I'll be back around five."

My mother was quiet that summer, I remember. Like Sophie, I had learned how best to avoid her, how best to sustain the suggestion that there were no children in the house at all. We saw her at meals, when we ate at home, and I would sometimes pass her in the hall or if I was coming out of the kitchen. She almost never came upstairs. I can't think of a time, after the baby died, that I saw her on the first floor of the house. And mostly, of course, she remained in her dry drawing room, filtering the daylight through heavy curtains and sitting, or walking, whichever fitted best with her moods.

She was not a mystery to me then; she had none of the romance of a mystery. She was just a part of life, one that was as much a background to my childhood as the wallpaper of the corridor or the smell of a classroom at school. The shadow she cast across us was never properly visible to me. When she died, I suppose I thought about her more in five days than, previously, I might have thought in five years. The mysteries that conspired to create my mother were never handed down to me; if they had been, I would have a clearer and more complete picture of my life, and of Sophie's, than I have. And so my mother, who in life had seemed to impinge upon my existence only in the most tenuous ways, attained a mystery in death, when I finally realized that the questions she raised would never be answered. She had married late, had children late, and my grandmother was dead before I was born. I have no knowledge of her whatsoever. Perhaps Ol' Grady evolved from some early precursor of which I know nothing; perhaps he had survived, in spirit, for generations before Sophie broke the chain and killed him. It is unreasonable to set limits or boundaries to a story when that story is, in essence, the lives of people. The only limits are those imposed by our ignorance.

It was at about this time that the real change in Sophie began to become evident. She had already found that clothes, and manner, could affect the image she created in the minds of others. This was something she was able to control, and she studied it as intensively as she could. But the chance combinations that go to make up physical beauty—the fluke that delineates between attractiveness and unattractiveness—was never accessible to her. And so she ignored them, and perhaps she, too, was surprised at what had been happening, gradually, over the past three years or so. Where Sophie had been unremarkable, neither noticeably plain nor noticeably pretty, she had begun to change. At first she simply crossed the line from unremarkable to pretty. There was a lengthening in her face and jaw that made sophistication of her childish pensiveness, and some unqualifiable alteration in the lines of her cheeks that left her with a striking maturity. She was never conspicuous, but a second glance at her was more than enough to establish her as pretty; and if you looked longer, you could see the first indications that she would turn into a beautiful young woman.

I noticed much of this for one good reason, I think. It was that, ever since she had dressed up in jeans and a shirt in her bedroom and made me believe for a moment that she was somebody else, I had been attuned to the way she looked. In this respect I was probably the best placed observer, having seen her every day throughout our childhood together, and having her face firm in my memory.

I always remember it as the summer that Sophie went away. In reality, though, it was more complex than that; I would have done better to call it the summer that Sophie moved on—moved on into something new, and out of what she left behind. I think she saw it this way as well, no matter what she said to me; it must have been impossible for her not to. The summer days we spent playing were the end of something that had started with my birth and lasted for eleven years. That the turning of a calendar page could tear it all apart so easily was difficult to believe, and I didn't want to believe it. I wanted her there for longer. Until I was ready, I told myself; I wasn't ready for this just yet. But there was another part of me—a silent, secret part—that was waiting without fear or pain, and with something like hope. The weeks of the holiday passed both slowly and quickly, and I no longer knew what I felt, nor what I wanted to feel.

Towards the end of the summer, preparations had to be made for Sophie's move to her new school. My mother returned one day with a trunk she had bought in the town, and Sophie and I carried it upstairs to her room. Her face was thoughtful, almost sad, when we had set it down on her bed. It was large, a dark blue colour, with brass corner pieces and a brass lock. Sophie opened it, and the inside was lined with tartan paper. It smelled strange, unfamiliar.

"There's too much room in here for my stuff," she said. "It'll all slop about."

We stared at the trunk together, and didn't know what else to say.

There was still a fortnight or so left to us, however; the countryside was ours to use, and we spent hardly any time indoors, unless it was in the barn. There, safely enclosed in our hidden room, we sat for hours, reading or talking, with Sophie telling me what she imagined her new school would be like, the things she might do there. I listened with a strangely potent mixture of envy and sadness, seeing her on the brink of another world, about to move off into it and leave me behind.

"You sure you won't get bored with me?" I said. "When you're at your big school."

She blinked, and a curious expression came over her face that I didn't remember having seen before.

"Don't be stupid," she said. "Of course I won't. You know I love you, don't you?"

"Yeah," I said, unable to meet her eyes.

"Well, I *do*," she said, fiercely. "And don't you forget it, OK?"

"OK," I said, and managed to smile.

"I'll always be around. You'll get bored with me, if you're not careful."

"No I won't."

"Then I won't, either. Do we have a deal on that?"

I grinned reluctantly. "I s'pose so."

"All right. So stop moping."

"OK," I said.

We walked the lanes and tracks that spider-webbed across the hills around our house, and we gathered flowers and sang songs. Once or twice we sat and watched the sun go down over the trees to the west, and we climbed to peer into birds' nests and threw stones into the middle of the stickleback lake. Sophie read to me from *Alice* and we made daisy chains, looping them over the branches of a rowan tree that grew by the path when we had done with them. In the evenings, if we were sitting across from one another at the supper table with my mother looking on coldly, we would exchange knowing glances, sharing the knowledge of what we had done—things that she would never know about, and in all likelihood would never have understood.

In this manner time passed quickly. But each night, before I was overtaken by sleep, I would think that the day past had narrowed the distance to the beginning of the next school year. I would be in a new class, enjoying some of the prestige associated with being in the lower of the two senior year groups, but not yet faced with the pressures and expectations of the final exam year. Also, though, I would have to walk home after school on my own, and there would be no one there to suggest a visit to the quarry or the holly bush. For the first time in my life, I realized, I would actually be alone.

"How long is it now?"

She looked at her watch, checking the date. "Another eight days. Stop counting the minutes, will you? Like I said, it's not the end of the world." But she sounded sad when she said it.

No, I thought to myself; but it will be the beginning of a different world, for me as well as for you. It was a complicated thought, although it had surfaced in my mind neatly packaged, as though it had rested there for some time, gathering itself. I turned it around and looked it over, and knew that it was true. I sighed.

"I guess not," I said.

# thirteen

"**M**attie?"

I looked up from where I had been staring into the stream. "Yeah?"

"Want to go for a walk? There are some—there are one or two things I want to do."

"OK," I agreed readily. It was evening, about five o'clock, and tomorrow my mother would take Sophie to the station, put her on a train, and watch her disappear towards a place she had only seen once before. "Where are we going?"

"Places," Sophie said vaguely. "All the normal places. OK?"

"OK," I said again, and got up to follow her. I had noticed something odd about her speech, a hesitancy that was unusual for Sophie. She sounded as if she was uncertain of something, which was so unlike her as to be disturbing. We went back to the house, and I found my anorak. "Are we going to be gone for long?"

"Yeah," she said. "Probably. Wait a minute." She stopped in the downstairs hallway, head on one side, thinking for a moment. Then she said to herself, "Yes, that's all." She looked at me and grinned. "Sorry. Just sorting things out. Tomorrow's the big day, after all."

I nodded. "Yeah."

"Well, come on, then." We left by the front door, and immediately turned to pass the house and head up the hill towards the quarry. The late afternoon sunlight was still warm on the side of my face as we climbed the hill, and there was the familiar sound of birds calling in the wood. As we made our way up, Sophie hummed a tune to herself, something that I recognized from a long time before.

"What's that?"

"Hmm? What?"

"The song."

"Oh, right. Don't you remember? 'The Raggle Taggle Gypsies.' "

"You sang that to me before," I said, doubtfully.

"That's right. When you were little. Must have been—what, five or six years ago. You're getting grown up."

"You are," I said.

"Doesn't mean I forget things, though," she said seriously.

As we neared the crest of the hill, I said, "Sophie?"

"Yeah?"

"When are you grown up?"

She raised her eyebrows. "What, for good? I don't know. I think it's different for different people. Some people take longer than others. Do you mean your body, or the way you think?"

"Both, I think," I said.

"Your body's just about finished by the time you're sixteen or seventeen, roughly," she told me. "Or at least, it doesn't change so much after that. Your mind's different, though. I don't know about that. I think we're expected to grow up when we're about eighteen, so most of us do. Perhaps if we were expected to grow up at fourteen, we'd grow up then instead." She drew breath, and then laughed. "Where have all these complicated thoughts come from, anyway?"

"I don't know," I said. "I got thinking about it last night."

The woods were a warm green, thick with low sunlight and swimming with insects. Instinctively, I started to head for the track down to the quarry floor, but Sophie stopped me.

"Let's go over here, first," she said, pointing to the left. We scrambled through the undergrowth until we came to the fence; we had approached the quarry from the south side, the side where the cages were, where I had once stood and thought about launching the model Spitfire I had built a year ago. Wondering what Sophie was doing, I followed her as she climbed over the fence at much the same place that I once had, where a fallen branch had dragged the palings and tangles of barbed wire down to ankle level. I stepped over after her and we stood together on the four or five feet of turf between the fence and the lip of the quarry. I could see the far end of it, where the tall weeds had grown strong and green in the sun, curling purple flowers at their heads.

"This was the very first secret place," Sophie said, looking down. "Do you remember? I brought you here and we sat in the sun and I waved flowers for you, and drew pictures on slate."

I thought back. "I don't think so," I said.

"You were pretty small. I had to carry you up here. Took me most of an afternoon, but I wanted you to see. I used to come here on my own, before that. And then you got older, and you had that craze with fossils."

"Yeah," I said. "I gave you a fossil, once."

"I've still got it. Come forward a little." We went farther towards the edge, and more of the quarry came into view. The centre of the quarry floor, where we normally sat, with its familiar rocks and boulders, was stretched out below us, the pale colour of the slate in shadow now from the declining sun. There was only a crescent of light on the east side, at the top, where the track cut down, and even this was slipping surely away as we talked.

Sophie said, "Will you come here? When I'm away?"

"I don't know. Should I?"

"Yeah, if you like. It belongs to both of us. It's pretty good, sometimes, to just sit somewhere and know that no one's going to find you. You need that, sometimes." She exhaled gently. "People can get—very difficult to deal with. And secret places make that easier. You understand?"

"I think so," I said.

"If you don't right now, you probably will one day soon. Anyway." She shaded her face and looked across to where the sun was starting to dip below the line of the hills. "Come here a sec."

I edged forward a little way, until I was level with her. She was only a couple of feet from the edge.

"Be careful," I said. "It cuts under all round here."

"I know. I want you to see as much of it as possible. It's safe enough." She took a step back, behind me, and rested her hands on my shoulders. "This place is just as much yours as it is mine," she said. "It doesn't matter if you can't remember when you first came here. Don't let anyone else come here, OK?"

"OK," I said. I was only a foot from the edge, and the drop to the quarry floor made my head reel. "Can we go back now?"

Sophie shifted her hands a little on my shoulders.

"Can we?"

Gently, she pulled me back a little way. "Yeah. I just wanted you to see it. Come on."

We made our way round to the path down, and followed it until we were standing in the middle of the darkened quarry.

Moving to one side, I could just see the tops of trees flaming in the light of the dying sun, but otherwise the empty quarry was a lake of shadows.

"I want to write something," Sophie said. She went off to the cage and took the bag from beside it, returning to sit down next to me. "Won't take long."

I kicked stones from place to place, looking up at the rim of the quarry where we had been standing minutes before. Directly below that point was one of the cages; I charted the motion of an imaginary rock falling from that point, and then went over and stood on the place where I guessed it would fall. Looking up, the dark earth of the grass overhang was visible, a continuous flange running along the top of the rock. Looking back over to Sophie, I saw that she had finished her writing and was packaging up the books again. She really hadn't taken long; I was surprised.

"Shall I take the bag back?" I asked, when I had rejoined her.

"No," she said slowly. "No, I'm doing it this time." She thumped the bag with her hand, and the tin inside made a muffled noise. "You want any of the fossils in here?"

"No thanks," I said.

"Yeah, I thought not. We're done with this stuff now, I think." She walked briskly across to the farthest cage with me following. We stopped just outside it, and again I felt that queasy distaste in my stomach at the smell of it. In shadow, you could see hardly any distance into it at all. The thick iron bars and the huge padlock, thick with verdigris, stood mute sentinel.

I noticed that Sophie's breath was coming quite quickly, as if she had run a short distance. The light was such that I couldn't be sure, but I thought that her face was pale.

"Right," she said quietly. Holding the bag in one hand, she worked it between the bars of the cage until it was hanging freely inside. I had a sudden, horrible vision of something rushing up to the bars from the inside to snatch at it, and felt my heart hammer abruptly in me. Sophie pushed her whole arm through, then swung the bag back and forth several times before letting go. It sailed a long way into the darkness, and there was a muted clatter as it fell among the beer cans and loose rocks of the cage. Sophie withdrew her hand carefully, rubbing streaks of rust from the sleeve of her anorak.

"That's taken care of," she muttered, more to herself than to me, it seemed. Then, more brightly, "Come on. I promised you a walk, didn't I? Let's get out of here."

I glanced back at the cage as we walked away from it. The opening was dark and silent, and when I swallowed, my throat was dry.

"You said that you'd read the quarry books," I say.

"That's right. I went back there—afterwards—with the key to the cage. They were still there, in the same place."

"You had the key?"

"Yes." He says nothing more.

I search for something else to ask. "Why did you go back?"

"I wanted to be sure about everything. To find out as much as possible about you. To try to get to know you."

"Why?"

He exhales. "Because I'd realized, by then, that I hardly understood my sister at all. I'd thought that I did, but I was wrong. I wanted to start again, to have another chance. . . . After you went away, it became important to do that. There was nobody to stop me, so I went back to the quarry, and I read the quarry books." He smiles slightly. "It was a foul afternoon, drizzling, really cold. It seemed appropriate, somehow."

"When was this?" I ask.

"When I was sixteen. I'm not sure why it took so long. I knew where they were, after all. Part of it was just—recognizing that I needed to see them, and part of it was working up the courage. I didn't really want to go back. I hadn't been back to the quarry since that night."

"Not at all?"

He closes his eyes. "Not at all."

"Tell me about when you did go back, then," I say.

As I walked out along the road to our house, things hardly looked different, although I hadn't been this way for five years. The sky was thick with clouds, and I could see a grey veil of rain drifting across the hills towards the horizon. I followed the road out of town, taking the same route that Sophie and I had walked every day after school. Fallen leaves were banked heavily to either side of the road, under the hedgerows. As I walked by the farm, the black, skeletal struts of the barn stood up sharply. There was a line of barbed wire across the top of the gate, and a notice warning of unsafe buildings. Slates had been torn from the roofs by the storms of several winters, and thick clumps of browning nettles rustled against the walls.

By the time I left the road and started up the hill towards the wood, the first drops of rain had started to strike the ground. The path, tight up against the stone wall, seemed much smaller than I remembered it. The rain began properly, then. It fell without much wind, slanting down into the hillside, until running water was carving little gullies in the path as I watched. The coat I was wearing was waterproof, but made not much difference; rain ran down my neck and soaked my shirt, and my shoes and the bottoms of my trouser legs were stained dark with mud. I continued up the hill, feeling the cold now through my clothing.

When I reached the woods I ploughed on through the under-growth, trying to ignore the tugging brambles that had trailed across the path. Although it was the middle of the afternoon, the woods were as dark as dusk, lit by eerie storm light, hissing and thrumming with the falling rain. The way down the shallow side of the quarry was slippery, the shale loosened and treacher-ous. I made it halfway down without falling, and then had to sprint the rest of the way as the rocks began to shift and slide under my feet. I ran out a little way across the floor of the quarry and then turned to see what damage I had done; a delta-shaped slide of loose debris had slumped four or five feet down, and there were little streams of loose pebbles and pale mud running from it.

The quarry floor was dancing with the rain. It was falling more heavily now, so that the cages were almost obscured, re-duced to dark blurs through the curtain of heavy drizzle. My hair was plastered down against my head, and I found I was shivering. I rubbed my arms against myself as I headed towards the cages. Once there, I grabbed the bars to steady myself, and, automati-cally, found myself looking to the right of the cage, at the place beneath the overhang where the quarry bag had always been. It wasn't there any longer, of course. That was why I was here.

With numb fingers I fumbled in my pocket for the key-ring. The padlock on the cage door was, when you looked at it closely, relatively new compared to the iron bars. I unlocked it, took it off and set it on the ground. Then I shook myself, and heaved. The door was very rusty, and the hinges did not give easily. I set my foot against the rock of the quarry wall and, braced, pulled again, using my legs and back as well as my arms. There was a sound of tearing metal, a low shrieking, and the cage door came open. I rubbed my hands on my trousers, leaving ochre stains, and picked up the rucksack. The rain kept falling in the quarry as I shrugged at the heavy material of my soaked clothing, and ducked my head as I stepped inside the cage.

The quarry bag had fallen quite a long way back inside. I took out my torch, set it down on the floor, and into its triangle of light I set the tin. The metal had rusted thoroughly. I squatted among the rubbish on the floor and stared around me. The floor was littered with fragments of glass and old cans, gaping with rust holes. The cage, from inside, was more like a tunnel, leading back into the rock face and sloping upwards slightly. The rock was dry.

The lid was difficult to prise off after all this time. I managed it in the end by turning it on its side and stamping on it, forcing the metal out of shape so I could secure a fingerhold. Inside, the plastic bags were intact. Sophie had tied their necks, that last time, and the books appeared well preserved. I took them out, tucking them inside my coat carefully, and put the tin back in the quarry bag. The sound of rain outside was growing lighter.

I picked up the torch, and shone it for a second down into the throat of the cage. I could just make out the curve of rock where the tunnel angled to the right. I shivered, and turned again towards the quarry.

As I had thought, the rain had slackened. The quality of light was different. I set my shoulder to the cage door and pushed, sending miniature avalanches of slate cascading down from my feet. I rested against the bars for a moment, and then retrieved the padlock, locking it firmly into place. It was a solid, heavy-duty model, far stronger than the cheap ones that secured the other cages.

I checked the quarry books were safe, grimacing at the discomfort of my sodden clothing, and then headed off back across the quarry. Above me, the first grey hints of late afternoon sunlight were visible through the clouds.

•  •  •

"I translated them all," he says. I have come to recognize the vacant, tranquil expression that comes over him at times like this. It shows he is trying to deal with something that is difficult for him. I keep quiet and let him talk without interrupting.

He says, "The earlier codes were the easiest. I expected that, of course. The later ones took much longer. You kept changing them. It's astonishing, I suppose—the way you kept them all in your head. You used to write them without even thinking." He stops, turns his head slightly. "That's strange. You know, I can't ever remember you reading things from the quarry books. You never looked back in them. You just wrote things. I never thought of that before." There is a long pause, and it starts to look as if he is not going to speak.

I say, "Maybe that's what they were for. Just to write things down."

"Yeah. I think so, too. That's how it felt, when I read them."

Carefully, I try to draw him out a little more. "What did you think? When you'd read them?"

He doesn't look at me. His eyes focus instead on the dying candle, and he gets up to light a new one from it, kicking the spent stub from the floorboards and rolling it absently into a corner of the room.

And I realize. Abruptly, without warning, I realize, and I am suddenly terrified. Something inside me freezes. I say nothing. I try to show nothing. But the fragments are falling into place, and I can see at last the picture that they create.

He is talking again, but I can hardly hear him over the rushing in my ears.

Translating the quarry books was painstaking, and although I used every spare hour that I had, it still took two months before

I had finished the last of them. Because of what they were, I had to use one of my secret places so that there was no chance of anyone discovering them, which limited the opportunities I had to work on them still further.

There were things in them that I had suspected, and other things I had not. I guessed that they began when Sophie was five or so. I made little sense of the earliest entries; they referred to things that I had never heard of, and people I had never known. She mentioned me often; it surprised me. And then, as the entries progressed, I began to notice references to things I recognized.

> *bad dreams still i try to make things ok but theres only 1 way to do that properly which will have to wait shes getting worse and i wont have her scaring him hes too small to know now but i will tell him someday*

She talked about Ol' Grady, and for a time I thought that perhaps I had the answer to the mystery of how she killed him. But the only entry in the quarry books that came close to a description of that incident was, itself, mysterious, and I never understood it fully. It was too short—perfunctory—almost as if she was unwilling to talk about it.

> *longer than i thought so i had to wait two days ago when mattie was asleep i did it so now ol greedy is back where he used to be i wish i could finish it now but i am too young we both are*

The last phrase I did understand, and it chilled me.

The Sophie of the quarry books was different to the Sophie I'd known; revealed starkly, through words, she lost all her humour and warmth and became perplexing, unnerving, even alien. More than at any other point, I realized just how right Andy had been when he told me she was not normal. The Sophie of the quarry books was too deliberate, her actions too sharp. I began to feel that I had known her hardly at all. She had inhabited a different world; things had happened, after I was asleep at night, that I had never known about. As I read the quarry books, I found myself reliving events that had been buried for years.

*its going to be anyway last night i waited very late so they were all in bed and at 4 i went down the hall and downstairs to see if they were asleep and they were so i went upstairs and did it i didn't want to but it was important everything would have come apart otherwise strange how it felt very warm when i touched it and quite soft so i stroked it with my fingers keeping calm and it moved just a little i was very quiet i shut the door before i started so then i knew i was going to do it properly now and i was breathing quickly i knew from the biology books where to touch where the opening was so i rested my hand there on it with my fingers where soft places were it was very dark but i could see all right and then i did it and squeezed as hard as i could very hard with my hand on the soft places and then it moved a lot and its eyes came open but it didnt make any sound when i finished i could see the dents in its head where the books said the openings were when it was over and not moving i checked the door again and stroked it some more and closed its eyes so it looked like it was sleeping and wiped the spit from its mouth where it had come out and it had wet itself but i left that i opened the door and went back to my room and waited for them to find out then i slept*

I got to know her through the entries in these coded diaries—got to see our childhood through her eyes for the first time. So I understood that she had done everything not out of impulse, or because of perverse pleasure, but in order to protect the two of us. Sophie, far more than I, was aware of the threat that the rest of the world posed. She disguised certain things, like her careful masking of her own abilities, and she anticipated others, like her decisive experiments with adolescence. And some, intrusions that she saw as endangering the two of us, she dealt with. To begin with, when I read these entries, I was horrified; but eventually—when I had read them again and again—I began to understand. To understand Sophie wasn't easy, because the quarry book writings made no concessions, no explanations, no excuses. I thought at first that this was because Sophie had never intended anyone else to see them. I was wrong in that, of course.

> *its because of that anyway steve and andy are working out better than expected do we credit fate with the coincidence i don't think so if only i can get a way into this i can use it and turn things around the important thing is to know beforehand i can use that i know i can the thing thats worrying me is the gap i mean how do you tell what something is before youre there you cant be sure ever so this is a good chance to try things at least ill know*

That passage I tagged; when I read it the first time, I assumed that Sophie was talking about her apprehension of the shift out of childhood, the concern that I had seen plaguing her all that last summer. That, after all, was why she had been reaching out, trying to gain a toehold in the next stage of her life. But after the second or third reading, I started to see a different meaning in the words, a meaning that suggested something strange and almost painful: that everything had been planned not just days, or weeks, but months in advance. When I realized that, I was overcome by a completely unexpected flood of emotion; a sort of awe and respect for Sophie—something I had never thought I would feel again.

Later on, I caught a section that was a clear reiteration of something she had written a very long time before.

*its going to but i havent forgotten what i said about her not for one day i remember each time mattie wakes up at night and each time i think of when i was little i said before that id do it and ive never lost hold of that just waited and waited on top of the old promise i make a new one it wont be easy for her she doesnt deserve that she never made it easy for mattie*

All the time, as I read them, I was searching for the place where Sophie had written, *But of course I do all of this for myself, not for anyone else.* There was no such line. No matter how many times I read the journals, I never found what I was looking for most. In the diaries, just as in everything else, Sophie and I were not distinguishable as separate people with separate identities; we were part of the same thing, part of each other, and whatever Sophie had done she had done for the good of the two of us. There was no way I was able to deny this, and it made no difference how hard I tried.

*and afterwards i said what would happen if he told anyone he was frightened in any case but this just scared him more it was so funny with him sitting there straw in his clothes and his trousers round his knees but i didnt laugh it wasnt*

*anything like i had thought really strange and it hurt a lot*
*but didnt last long weird to let someone do that anyway*

And, each time I read them through after the first time, it
was with the memory of the last page in my mind. The page that
Sophie had written in the quarry just before she threw the bag
into the cage, just before the summer ended and everything finished. I could remember her sitting there, writing, and knew
now that the reason she had been in a hurry, had taken so little
time over that last entry, was because she wasn't bothering with
the code. The message was simple enough, but I knew that no
one except me would have made sense of it.

*I could burn these, which would end everything. But there's*
*still the need for them, otherwise you wouldn't be holding*
*this now. I hope it explains some things. I hope you'll under-*
*stand. Once you've read these, you'll know everything. They're*
*for you. Only you know what they are.*
  *I hope everything's worked out.*
  *I love you always.*

The beating of my heart is very loud now. I have realized where
this is leading, and there is nothing I can do to stop it. And I
have finally pinpointed the gnawing, frustrating sense of near-
knowledge that has been in the back of my mind all along—
fixed it down, seen it clearly for the first time. The spent candles
in the corners of the room. I should have realized earlier.

There is nothing left but to carry it through. He said that he
had never never got far enough, before; maybe, if I push him to
finish this—this time—it will change things. It *must* change
things. Because if it doesn't, then I know already where this will
end.

"I want to know, Mattie," I say. He looks at me, his eyes confused. I press on regardless of what he may be thinking. "I want to know everything about that night. All of it."

"I—I don't want to," he says, and his voice is child-like. It scares me. I have no idea what I am forcing him into.

"You have to tell me," I say. "Don't you think it's about time you told someone?"

"I don't know if I can."

I can't control the trembling in my voice when I speak. If he won't do this, then it is finished.

"Take me back to it," I say, trying to put as much force into the words as I am capable of. I feel drained. I know I am drawing on strength I don't have. "Take me back to the evening when Sophie took you to the quarry, at the end of the summer. The last evening. What happened, Mattie? Where did you go after that?"

"We went home," he says. He is telling the truth.

"Why did you go home?"

His face is contorted, his hands clenched white.

I say again, "Why did you go home, Mattie?"

He says, "We went home to see Mummy."

# fourteen

The quarry books were never clear about the hold that Sophie had over my mother. To a large degree, I don't even know whether it was based on any concrete foundation, or whether it was simply the result of a battle that Sophie had long since won. The relationship between the two of them was, from my point of view, generally irrelevant; as my childhood progressed, so my mother's part in it became smaller and smaller, until at the end she was hardly a person at all. Inhabiting her dusty, closed-up room for longer and longer periods of time, she had become so distanced from me that, for much of the time, I didn't consciously recognize that she was still there.

With Sophie, I suspect it was different. She saw more of my mother than I did, partly because Sophie acted as intermediary between Mummy and her shadowy household, and partly because Sophie took a limited interest in Mummy's world, for reasons that were only ever apparent to Sophie herself. It was never that my mother actively trusted Sophie with the everyday workings of our life, but rather that Sophie left her no alternative. After that night—for several years—I would look back over the rare occasions where I had seen any kind of contact between the two of them, and replay the incidents in my head, looking for details. Sophie had interceded for me that frightening afternoon when school was over and I had been on the brink of understanding the quarry books. Sophie, time and again, had extracted from my mother permission to do things or go places without, so far as I knew, ever revealing exactly what we were planning. And, at some time in the past, in the time when I was too young to know what was happening around me, Sophie had found out that Ol' Grady was still alive, and had dealt with him.

In the quarry books, there was scant reference to those times, and no reference at all to Sophie's memories of Ol' Grady. But she must have had memories—she had heard the name differently, and she recognized the shuffling, faceless figure the moment that I mentioned it had crept along the walls in my dream. With Sophie knowing all this, then, and telling me about it only when it became necessary for *my* benefit, it seems less unlikely that there were other things Sophie knew about, and remembered. Later, I found quarry book entries that made no sense to me, but which might have made sense if I had known all of Sophie's own story.

> *asking myself whether it was worth it but i think it is going to be one day we have to keep on reminding ourselves about next year and the year after that i need to have something back here i can use if it becomes important later on shes quite able to understand if i make it clear and that i think will be all the lever ill need*

And, later, there were passages where I could detect real emotion under the words. It was rare, in the quarry books, to find this; as rare as finding it in Sophie herself, who was so used to keeping her emotions locked away out of sight.

*in this family there are rules if you know the rules you can use them mummy thinks she knows the rules but she only knows half of them the half she sees i know them all and thats why were safe here if i wanted i could show her whats really going on*

As we walked back from the quarry that evening, I didn't know what Sophie was thinking. She was quieter than usual, almost withdrawn, and although when she spoke her voice was even and calm, I could tell that her mind was elsewhere. It may have been that she was reviewing some of the things written in the books she had just thrown away into the mouth of the cage, some of the things about control, about knowledge, about the unspoken and hidden rules in our family.

The sun was grazing the tops of the trees when we reached the house, and there was birdsong from the wood. It was a beautiful, light evening in late summer, and the pale turquoises and rose pinks of the sky were veiled with delicate and translucent clouds. I hadn't really thought where we would go after the quarry, but I was surprised to find that we were back in our own garden. Sophie wandered over to the stream and touched the water, then straightened up and smiled at me.

"Come on," she said. "There are some things we have to do." She led the way over the small bridge into the orchard. The sheds, in their familiar places, huddled under the trees. Sophie retrieved a key-ring from her pocket, sorted through the keys, and unlocked the shed where the skin of Ol' Grady was kept. The night when she had taken me out here to see it was still firm in my memory, but the terror had drained out of the place since then, and the old sou'wester, still hung on the back of the door, didn't have very much of the nightmares clinging to it anymore. Sophie took it down, looked it over, and slung it over her arm. I didn't say anything. We walked back down the garden together in silence.

When we were at the back door, she stopped. "You can wait here," she said. "I shan't be long."

"Where are you going?" I said.

"I'm going to talk to Mummy. Then we'll go to the barn, OK?"

I nodded.

Sophie said, "It'll be all right. Don't worry." She fingered the material of the coat thoughtfully. "I think she knows what's coming in any case."

"I don't want to wait here," I said.

"It's best," she told me. "Really. I shan't be long." She smiled a little, and went inside, taking the coat with her.

I waited a while, growing more and more uncertain. I knew what I wanted to do, but at the same time I was very afraid. In the end, I shrugged off my trainers, and, walking very slowly and quietly, crept through the kitchen and into the downstairs hall-way. The door to the drawing room was slightly ajar, and a thin sliver of light cut across the hall carpet. There was the sound of voices from inside, barely audible. I moved slowly closer, adrena-line making me tremble. I could just make out Sophie's voice. She sounded calm, in control, reasonable.

"We'll be gone about four hours, I should think," she said. "I'll phone Dad after that. I've got his number. That should be long enough for you."

Then my mother, her voice distorted and almost unrecog-nizable with hate. "You little cunt," she said.

"It may take a day or two to get things sorted out," Sophie went on. She didn't seem to have heard Mummy at all. "I've got money, so that should be OK. Mattie's pretty grown up now, you may have noticed."

"You're a monster," Mummy said, and then she spoke out loudly, and for an instant my heart lurched and I thought she was talking to me. "I have a monster for a child."

"Try to concentrate," Sophie said. "I really don't want to have to go through all this again."

"Monster," my mother said. Her voice was weaker, as if she had suddenly lost touch with her hatred. "I should have got rid of you when I had the chance."

"Your mistake," Sophie replied evenly. There was a pause. "You knew this was going to happen eventually. Four hours. It's generous. You've got more than enough time for regrets."

I heard the boards creak under the soft pile as Sophie turned. Quickly, I retraced my steps and put my trainers back on. A minute or so later, Sophie emerged from the house again. She no longer had Ol' Grady's coat with her.

"We'll go to the barn now," she said. "It's a beautiful evening."

"Yes," I said.

"How much of that did you hear?"

I blinked. "Not much. The last part."

She was thoughtful for a moment. "Well, it doesn't matter." She looked at me. "You're too young to understand," she said, her eyes fixed on mine.

"Yes," I agreed. "I'm only eleven."

She smiled. "Well done, Mattie," she said. "Now, let's move. It'll be sundown soon."

We set off across the fields together.

He stares at the wall behind me. "Sometimes I think maybe she was right," he says.

"Who?"

"Mummy. Objectively, I suppose she was. But it didn't seem that way at the time."

"Of course not," I say. "You were only a kid."

He frowns sharply. "What?"

"You couldn't know any better."

"What would you know about it?" he says. I try to smile.

"Quite a lot, I should think." I let him take that in for a second, and then go on. "What do you think you meant when you said you were only eleven?"

"I don't know what you're talking about," he says. He doesn't sound confused, though. He sounds angry, almost defensive.

"Yes you do. Sophie said you were too young to understand, and you agreed with her. But you didn't mean it, and neither did she. So tell me the truth, Mattie. Were you really only a kid? Is that excuse good enough any more?"

"I don't *know*," he shouts. Then, after a second, he takes control of himself again. "I don't know. Yes, actually, I do think it's a good enough excuse. I wasn't like her. I was pretty much normal, and I didn't understand half of what went on."

"I don't believe you," I say.

"It doesn't matter what you believe," he says wretchedly. He runs a hand through his hair. "You don't understand."

Abruptly, I realize that neither of us is maintaining the pretence that I am Sophie any longer. It strikes me with the force of a blow.

"I understand more than you seem to think," I say, desperate to fill the sudden silence. "You've told me enough, Mattie. Enough to know that you knew Sophie far better than you'd like me to believe. That's right, isn't it?"

"I really didn't know what was going on that night," he says. "It all happened too quickly. I wanted to go with her, but I was too scared. And I hardly heard anything outside Mummy's room."

"But you did know what she meant," I persist. "Isn't that right?"

He rubs his mouth, his eyes darting about the empty kitchen. Finally, he says, "Yes, I knew what she was talking about. Is that what you wanted to hear?"

"I only want to hear the truth," I say, although even as I speak the words I am not sure if I mean them. He swallows, stands up. The candle stubs are visible, pale as corpses, at the periphery of my vision. I try to ignore them.

"Really?" he asks, as if he has read my mind.

"I think so," I say. "I think we both need to hear it. Am I right?"

"Maybe."

"You haven't said this part before, have you?"

"No."

"I need to hear it, Mattie. Keep going. Go back to when you left the house. I want to know what happened."

His eyes are fixed in space, unfocused. From nowhere, the thought comes to me—based on something he said about Sophie—that he is seeing landscapes I will never know.

We walked on across the fields, taking care to stay by the dry-stone walls as much as possible, until we reached the lane that overlooked the farm. Again, as we had at the edge of the quarry, we stood and stared at it for a long while before going any farther. We had walked slowly, talking a little at intervals, and in the time it had taken us to go from the quarry to the farm the sun had sunk below the horizon. The sky to the west was still a ruddy orange, but the grass underfoot had gone grey-blue with darkness and there was no longer any sound of birds from the woods.

We followed the same route down to the farmyard as we had the first time we had come there, keeping the body of the barn between us and the lights of the village. The hinged panel swung aside easily, but inside the barn it was pitch dark.

"Wait a minute," Sophie said, and fumbled in her pocket. "Here we go." She struck a match, and I watched in fascination as she lit the stub of a candle. I recognized it at once as the brand we had bought to fill the small candle-altars in the holly bush. As the wick caught, a warm yellow radiance pooled out around us. Sophie's eyes gleamed. She walked over to the foot of the straw fort and sat down on a bale. I followed. She dug one finger into the tough straw and then wedged the base of the candle stub into the hole; an inch or so of wax protruded when she had finished.

"There," she said. I kept quiet, knowing what was happening.

We watched the motes of chaff dance in the candlelight, and I swung my feet against the side of the bale as the dribbles of wax ran on to the straw and set there, gradually cementing the candle in place. The flame eased its way downwards very slowly. Sophie's face was dreamy, her expression vague.

"This is a good place," she said. I nodded. "We never went in the farm buildings," she went on. "That might have been interesting. I think we did all right, though."

"I think so, too," I said.

"Do you mean that?" she asked.

"Yeah."

She smiled, a sad smile, which was unusual for her. "Thanks, Mattie. You're all right, you know. We both are." I watched as the flame sank slowly down.

She said, "I don't want to grow up, Mattie. I don't want to be like Mummy."

"You won't be like Mummy," I said. "You're different."

"Yeah. I know. But it's all the same thing, really."

"Do you want never to grow up?" I asked.

"What, like Peter Pan? No, I don't think so. It would get boring, don't you reckon? Like always eating the same food, every day, every meal. And always wearing the same clothes. I don't think I could stand that. You just have to make your decisions and get on with things."

The candle flame licked tentatively at the first wisps of straw, and a thick curl of white smoke slid up towards the distant ceiling of the barn. At last, she said, "It's time to go. There's one thing we have to do here."

Not comprehending, I followed her out. Behind us, the candle burned strongly, spreading, its growing flame seeming to challenge the barn's dark recesses. I said nothing; this was Sophie's time, and I knew it. We went to the open shed, and found again the iron bar with which we had struck the heads off the rivets. We took it to the barn doors, and there Sophie slid it through the chain, and twisted it around and around until it was pulled very tight. We took one end of the long bar each, and continued to turn it slowly, winding it still further. Sophie's knuckles were white where she gripped the bar. There was a sharp crack, and the tension slackened immediately. I let go of the bar, and looked in astonishment at the link of the chain that had burst; I picked up one of the two pieces that had dropped, and while Sophie went back to replace the bar, I examined the two sections of bright steel that had been revealed inside its brown casing. It was hot enough to make me swap it from hand to hand. I put it in my pocket, and helped Sophie slide the huge doors open. The candle was still burning steadily.

"That'll do," Sophie said. "Let's go up to the hill."

Neither of us looked back as we climbed the slope. We headed for the place on the outskirts of the wood where there was a fallen tree, and we sat on it and waited. The farm buildings lit up gradually as the light from the open doorway of the barn increased. We heard the distant sounds of crackling, and occasionally a short, metallic explosion, as of something giving way in the heat. The frame of the barn was wooden, and a section of the roof fell in, leaving a wide gap through which flames as tall as houses hooted and roared.

The whole hillside was lit with a strange, awful red, such as you might see in nightmares. We sat and watched, me kicking my feet, Sophie as still and quiet as a statue, until there was the sound of fire engines in the distance. We saw the flickering blue lights come tearing through the town, we saw them hose down the adjacent farm buildings and stand back to let the fire run its course. We waited for a long time, with the fire throwing our shadows out behind us.

"I shouldn't think there'll be much left," Sophie said.

"No."

"If there had been anyone in there, when it started, then I shouldn't think there'd be much left of them, either."

"Do you think Andy and Steven will find out?" I said.

"Yeah, they should do. You know where they live, don't you?"

"Yes," I said. She'd told me.

"Steven's a bright boy," she said, thoughtfully. "He'll know what to do. I had a talk with him."

"OK."

She sighed. "It's pretty, isn't it? I'd like to stay longer."

"We can, if you like," I said.

"No. We'd better get going. There's still a lot left to do."

We set off through the grass, heading up the hill. Behind us, the roaring of the fire could still be heard, even after we had walked around the shoulder of the land and the farm itself was out of sight. There were thin, low clouds in the sky, and over towards the village they were stained bloodred. Now and then glowing ashes would spiral down out of the night air to settle and die on the ground.

When we were at the outskirts of the woods, Sophie stopped, looking down the hillside to the dark outline of our house. There was a single light burning in the drawing room window. She shrugged slightly, turned, and went on ahead of me into the shadows.

He is on his feet again, nervously pacing the room. The boards creak every so often as he walks. When he speaks, he is hesitant, edgy, clearly upset by what he is telling me. All the time he seems to be looking beyond the walls of the room—and I suppose, in a sense, he is doing exactly that.

"You went back to the quarry," I say.

"Mm."

"Talk to me, Mattie. She took you back to the quarry. What then?"

"We sat down on the grass," he says.

"On the grass? Where?"

"Where we'd been before. By the rim of the quarry. We were too far from the fire to hear it, by then," he adds.

"OK, so she took you back to the quarry," I say. "What happened then? What did she say?"

He puts his palms flat against the far wall of the kitchen, leaning into it. "She said that there was some diesel in the shed where Ol' Grady was. That I should burn the holly bush, so that everything was taken care of. She wanted everything neat, everything sorted out."

"Why didn't she do it herself?"

"She said she was tired, and she didn't want to do any more. She said I'd got the idea by now in any case."

"Had you?"

"I thought I had. I thought she just wanted everything erased, so that there was nothing left of the secrets and so on."

I remember something from earlier. "It wasn't, though, was it? There were still secrets, even after the barn and the quarry books were gone."

"I know," he says, almost in a whisper. "I know."

"And what about you, Mattie? What happened to you? You went back and found the quarry books for a reason. What was it?"

I can see where his fingernails have scored the old plaster. His face is turned away from me, but I can hear pain in his voice when he speaks. "I had to know everything for certain. I had to be sure."

"You had to be sure of what you felt about her," I say. I try not to make it a question.

"I loved her. She was the most important thing in my world."

"She *controlled* your world, Mattie. Are you sure you loved her?"

"I loved her," he repeats, stubbornly.

"You hated her. You didn't know what you thought about her, so you went back to the quarry to make sure. That's right, isn't it?"

"I did *not* hate her," he says, turning round to look at me. I struggle, using my feet, to kick myself upright against the wall until I am standing. He is still talking, oblivious. "I just didn't understand her properly."

"She abandoned you," I say. The tape round my wrists is still tight. "You hated her because of that. What do you wish had happened, Mattie?"

"Nothing! I never hated her! You don't know anything about this. What you're saying makes no sense."

"Really?" I am shouting at him, now, trying to force the words through the sleeting memories that I cannot see. "How many have there been, Mattie? Which one am I?"

"I don't know what you mean!"

"How many before tonight? *How many Sophies, Matthew?*"

He rocks back on his heels, his eyes wide with shock. His mouth opens, but he seems unable to articulate anything.

"Which number am I? Look at all the candle stubs, Mattie. How many have there been, over the years? You'd got pretty used to this, hadn't you? Only you'd never told the whole story before, so this time it's been different. What did you do with them, Mattie?"

He shakes his head as if dazed. After a time, words come again, slowly, uncertainly. "I loved her," he says. "I know I did."

"How many Sophies?"

"I loved her. I just didn't understand. And I was too scared, when she asked me."

His face is terrible, knotted with conflicting feelings. He seems poised on the brink of something.

"I was too scared."

I hesitate, then take a step towards him. "Tell me what happened," I say. "Finish it."

He nods. "All right. It's time it was finished, I think."


We climbed the fence where the fallen branch had brought it to the ground. The little area of clear turf was dark, but we could see the lip of the quarry easily enough; the pale stone below reflected the faint light from the night sky. Above, in the gaps between the clouds, the stars were sharp and the moon half full. The woods rustled gently with night breezes. We had left the barn behind us: on the walk to the quarry, even the smell of smoke had been drawn out of our clothes. If we chose not to think about it, there was nothing to remind us of it.

"It's good, here," Sophie said. "I think I like this place best of all. It's always been special." She paused. "Do you think you'll come here again?"

"When you're away?" I said.

She raised one eyebrow. "Yeah, that's right."

"I don't know," I said, honestly. "It won't be the same."

"I suppose not. Oh, wait a minute." She searched through the pocket of her anorak. "Here. Keep hold of this for me, will you? I'll explain in a bit." She had taken out the key-ring I'd seen her with earlier, and unhooked a small grey key. I took it from her carefully.

"Hey," she said, sounding surprised. "Look what I found." She held out her hand a second time. In the palm was a round, dark medallion of some kind. "Do you recognize it?" she said.

"What is it?"

"It's your ammonite," she said. "The fossil you gave me. I kept it safe." She looked at it, weighing it. "Do you want it back?"

"No," I said. "I gave it to you. Keep it."

"Thanks." She didn't look up from it. "This was your best one, wasn't it?"

"I think so."

"Yeah. I think so, too. Thanks, Mattie."

"It's OK," I said, embarrassed.

"I wonder if I ever gave you anything like that in return," she said, half to herself.

"Lots of times," I said. It was a strange remark, and it had surprised me.

"I don't know," she said. "Sometimes it doesn't seem like that at all."

We sat quietly for a while, looking at the trees and the eerie shapes made by their branches and leaves against the sky. Sophie picked up a pebble and turned it around in her fingers before letting it drop to the grass. I pulled my anorak tighter around me.

"You cold?"

"No," I said.

She looked away again. "I'm not going away to school," she said. "You knew that, though."

I was silent.

"You knew that, didn't you, Mattie?"

I didn't know what to say.

"Anyway, I'm not. I've thought about it for a long time. This is all over, you know. It's all finished. The barn, the quarry, the house. Mummy. Us. Everything. It's all gone."

I found my voice at last. "Only because you made it finish," I said, and some of the hurt must have come through. She looked up at me, and her mouth was slightly open. The expression in her eyes was that of someone betrayed.

"I didn't make it finish," she said. "There's nothing I can do about it."

"You burned the barn," I said.

She blinked, and I realized she was blinking away tears. In eleven years, I had never seen Sophie cry. "It's over in any case, Mattie," she said. "That's just how things have turned out. I tried to find ways to change things, but I couldn't."

Again, I could find nothing to say to help her. When she realized I wasn't going to speak, she struggled on alone.

"It's not easy to put into words, Mattie. I don't know if I understand it all myself. But if I had gone away to school, and left you, it would have torn everything apart. *Everything*. It would have destroyed—everything." She was casting about in desperation for words that would make sense to me, but we both knew she wasn't succeeding.

In the end, I said, "You'll do the right thing. You always work things out."

She smiled slightly at that. "You're OK," she said again.

The wind moved slightly in the dark trees behind us. At the far end of the quarry, just visible, the stems of the tall weeds stirred and quivered. The ground underneath me was cold through my jeans.

"I want you to promise me some things," Sophie said.

"OK."

"In the back of the shed where we found Ol' Greedy there's a grey can. It's got diesel in it. Use it to burn the holly bush, OK? I can't be bothered, but it would make everything symmetrical at least. Will you do that?"

"Yes," I said.

"You're not sad, are you? Don't be sad, Mattie."

"I'm not sad," I said. I thought of the afternoons we had spent in the holly bush, with Sophie reading to me or telling me stories. Those afternoons didn't feel as if they belonged to me any more; they had somehow become the property of someone else, without my noticing. I didn't even feel jealous of whoever it was that had inherited them from me.

"What else?" she said to herself. "You'll have to call Daddy, of course. I should think he'll probably be quite pleased, once he stops being shocked and so on. He always liked you, you know."

I hadn't known; I said nothing.

"He'll manage everything," she went on. The words were very measured, very careful, and I got the feeling that she was trying hard to cover up what she was really thinking. "Well. That's about it, I think."

"Sophie? I still don't understand."

She reached out, took my hand and squeezed it tightly. "Don't worry," she said. "Everything's going to be OK, you'll see. Trust me."

He hits his forehead with the heel of his palm. "Why did she say that? That everything would be all right? She must have known it wouldn't be true."

"Maybe she thought it was the best thing to say," I suggest.

"Do you think she really meant it?" He is almost pleading.

"I don't know. I don't think she would have lied to you."

"Why do you say that?"

"She loved you too much," I say. His eyes widen as he stares at me. I keep talking, trying to get the sense of what I am feeling across to him. "She loved you too much, Mattie. She didn't really have any choice. Things were always extremes with Sophie, always superlatives. I don't think she had any control over *that*. She couldn't change the way her mind worked. And if she had been able to, and had made herself average, then she wouldn't have been able to look after the pair of you. She needed to be different."

"I couldn't believe she'd leave me behind," he says.

"I want you to promise me some things," she said. "Will you do that?"

"Yes," I said.

"OK. Good. Listen carefully." She outlined the events of the evening as they would eventually be told, and I sat in front of her on the turf taking in the details dutifully. It was all easy enough to remember.

"You're going to have to wait a while, at home," she said. "To make sure everything is timed right. Do you think you can do that?"

"I think so," I said. "I'll try."

"That's great. That's all that's necessary."

Overhead, the sky was becoming thickly sown with stars as the clouds pulled away. The thin breeze of earlier had dropped, and we were left sitting in a strange, unearthly calm. The night, through the woods, seemed very deep.

She looked at me, her face serious. "Mattie?"

"Yeah?"

"You'll be OK, won't you?"

I didn't know what to say. I didn't even know if I was frightened or not. "Yes," I said. It was the only thing I could think of.

Sophie looked at her watch. "One last thing," she said. "You're going to have to be very brave, and do exactly what I tell you. You've still got the key?"

I nodded, and showed it to her.

He walks over to the door into the garden. He appears to be thinking; he is frowning, and his hands twist against one another involuntarily. There is a long pause. Light is seeping through the cracks in the window boards; pale, early dawn light, but light even so. The room is a ghostly grey. The candle burned out unnoticed while he was speaking.

I am left here staring at a man I hardly knew yesterday. Overnight, everything I thought about him has been turned around, thrown apart; he isn't the person I took him for at all. But, at the same time, I am no longer afraid of him. I'm not sure why. It's as if we came through all this together. In a sense, I suppose, we both have. And, strangely, understanding what he has been saying has meant thinking, at least a little, the way that

Sophie thought. I don't yet know what to make of this—don't know whether it frightens me or not.

He turns, comes over to me. For the first time since he hit me, hours ago, he stands close to me. He hit me, of course, for not being her. Or for saying so. I'm no longer sure which. But we've done this by the rules he set, and still it has come out my way.

"Give me your hands," he says quietly. I hold them out to him, taped wrists crossed over one another, and he takes a pocket knife from his trousers and cuts the tape. I pull my hands free, wincing as the adhesive parts from my skin, and rub them together, feeling them tingle.

"Thanks."

He stands up again, walks back over to the door. There are bolts at the top and at the foot, and he pulls them back. With his shoulder he forces the door open, shoving it outwards, and for the first time I see the garden at the back of the house. It's unruly and tangled, but I recognize it nevertheless. It is perhaps slightly smaller than I imagined it. He stands looking out, and, shakily, I get to my feet and go over to join him.

"There's the holly bush," he says, pointing. He's right; it is starting to grow out again, fresh shoots rising from the base of the trunk. "I did just as she said, found the can and burnt it down when I got back to the house." He sighs. "I was sad to see it go, I suppose, but by then I wasn't really caring what happened. It was several hours later. A lot had happened."

"I know," I say.

"When I got home, I waited, just like she'd said. I went to her room, and sat on her bed. I must have been there for over an hour. In the end, I didn't even have to call anyone; somebody must have seen the fire in our garden, because suddenly there

were cars and a fire engine and so on all over the lane. They
found Mummy first, I think, because they wouldn't let me near
the drawing room. Then the police turned up. They wanted to
know where my father was, and where Sophie was. I said I didn't
know where my father was, but that I had his number. I was so
tired I was almost asleep on my feet, but they wouldn't let me
sleep; I don't suppose I could have in any case. When they'd
called my father, they started asking where Sophie was again.

"I said she'd gone to the barn earlier on. When I saw the fire
from my bedroom I had gone out over the fields to see where
she had got to, but she wasn't there. They all looked at each
other, and they looked at the mud on the carpets from my trainers, and presumably they saw how I looked as well, because
somebody carried me outside to an ambulance and sat me in it
while they went on trying to understand what had happened in
the house. Someone else brought me a drink, but I didn't want
it. It was coffee, from a thermos. I wanted to say that I only had
orange squash at night, but I couldn't really make the words
come clear. I think I did sleep for a while, then.

"They waited a long time for my father to arrive, but when
he didn't, they took me to hospital. I don't think anyone could
think what else to do with me. They gave me pyjamas and put
me in a bed, and I fell asleep for most of the day. When I woke
up, there were ashes on the pillow from my hair. People asked
me questions, later on, about what had happened. I remembered to ask them if they'd found Sophie yet, and they said no,
that I should try to rest, that they'd talk to me about it later. I
could see the looks of worry on their faces as they tried to find
ways of telling this little boy that his sister had been burned to
death while playing in a barn, that they hadn't even been able to
find her body.

"It was my father who, in the end, had to tell me about Sophie,

and about Mummy. I sat up in bed, with pillows propped up behind me, and listened in silence. My father had had to come
back to England from America, where he had been working. I
remember a tall man walking into the room where my bed was,
wearing a clean white shirt. He looked tired, but his face was
pleasant enough. There had been strangers coming in and out of
my room all day, so it was only when he came close to me that I
realized he was my father. I recognized his smell. He sat down
on the edge of the bed and told me what had happened. He did
it very well, I think. It can't have been easy for him.

"That's all. This house was put up for sale, but nobody ever
bought it. Too many people knew what had happened here, and
word gets round about houses that have harboured suicides. It'll
be here till it falls down, I expect."

I look at him, his face pale in the early light. "What about
me?" I say.

"You're safe," he says. "I don't know why. You're more like
her than anyone I've met since. I never thought I'd tell anyone
all of that."

"Why all the other Sophies, Matt?" I ask.

He shrugs, rubs his eyebrow with the side of his hand. "I
wanted to kill her, later on," he says. "I wanted to do it properly.
Even once she'd gone, she was still in control."

"Ah," I say. "That's how it was."

"She never really left," he continues. "I thought, maybe if
I killed her properly, she wouldn't keep coming back. But it
didn't work. It never worked."

"Where are they?" I say. I can't help myself.

"Around," he says vaguely. Of course, this is the only room of
the house that I have seen. He raises his eyes to meet mine. "I
could have killed you," he says.

"I know."

"Don't worry. You're safe now. I told you that. But I want something from you."

"What?" I ask.

"Come on," he says, and takes me by the hand. We set off across the matted lawn of the garden, still sodden with the rain from the storm, towards the hill.

# fifteen

It is not cold; the air moves very gently against my face, and underfoot the ground is dry. There is no sound. In the woods on the hill there was birdsong as we walked, but it has faded and vanished. The morning sunlight, rising above the trees, has vanished. The glistening bushes and wide, deep puddles have vanished. The world has shrunk down, condensed, focused itself here into a small space in which I am kneeling. The light is dim. There are candles back in the house, on the windowsill, and the candle stubs of many evenings scattered across the floor, but I have no light here except the little that filters around the corner.

It is almost beautiful. The floor is clear of the grit and debris that litters the entrance, and the roof, though low, is roughly arched and nearly symmetrical. The alcove is almost like a small altar in a corner of a church. The floor slopes upwards gradually from the entrance, then turns sharply right, widening a little some five yards farther in to form this space. It is calm here; peaceful. Everything that has been told seems such a long way away.

What is most strange is that I am here at all. As Mattie and I walked up the hill in the sunlight, I felt curious emotions stir in me; a sense of exhilaration, of triumph. The walk was difficult. My legs were weak and sometimes unstable, from tiredness, and many hours of sitting in one place, but not from fear any longer. Of all the Sophies there had been, none had managed to pull Mattie through the whole story, shown him everything that had happened, made him face it all. It occurred to me then, looking at it all, that perhaps this would never have happened had I not been, in some way, like Sophie; and while the thought should, perhaps, have repulsed me, instead I found it strangely invigorating. I felt I knew Sophie now, and I knew her to be strong. Mattie had always been weaker than her. I had looked for Sophie inside myself, and she had helped me through.

"I've seen the place where the branch broke the fence," I say, pleased that my voice is still level and pleasant. "The patch of grass. It's really very small. I suppose two children could sit there and talk, though." I think to myself. "He never actually told me what happened. Well, that's not quite true. He told me *what* happened, just not *how*. One last secret."

At the foot of the end wall of the cage there is a low shelf, just eight inches or so off the ground. It looks as if it's a natural part of the rock. There are some holes drilled at intervals in the face above which I assume were originally for explosives. All long ago abandoned, long ago forgotten.

Sophie is curled up there, hands pressed together in front of her, knees drawn up. Her red anorak is almost black in the dim light. I can't see her face very well, but then I am not trying to; it has been many years. And besides, I know already what she looks like. "He really loved you," I say. I think it is true, as well. "I suppose I'm the only person who knows you, apart from him."

I wondered, when I first saw her, how it had happened. The truth came slowly, but it made sense. It's the only way it could have happened. And so I am left with a mind too full of pictures,

pictures that I cannot confirm; Sophie asking Mattie to come with her, and he being too afraid. Mattie following her instructions carefully, walking away from the quarry through a night still stained red from the barn fire. Mattie in a hospital bed, holding the key to the quarry cage tightly in one hand, wondering. The days passing, and Sophie going further back into the darkness, finally falling asleep here where I have found her. I don't know that it was like this, or why she should have wanted it this way, but I can't help thinking, can't help it now. Especially now.

"He kept the key," I say. "All those years, just like you kept the ammonite." She is so peaceful, so strong, so enduring. If only I had been more like her. If only.

"You gave him the template," I say. "The key, the secret place. But you were the only one who really knew him. I should have seen that. He said it often enough. You were the only one that knew him, and he was the only one that knew you. I should have noticed. I noticed the candles, but I didn't notice that." I stop. I think I am talking too much. She wouldn't like that; it is a sign of panic, and I am not going to panic. Sophie is quiet.

"I knew you were here," I say. "That's really why I came. I came because I promised Mattie, but really I came because I wanted to see you." I smile at her. "He gave me the key to the cage. I've got it here." I take the key out of my pocket and hold it out tightly. She doesn't need to see it, of course, but I do it anyway. "He told me where you were. I was—he said I was different. He said I had taken him through it, and no one had done that before. Of course, I knew that. I knew I was as strong as you."

I put the key back. I don't know why I keep hold of it. It's a small, grey key, just like Mattie described Sophie giving him. Just before you reach the alcove where Sophie lies sleeping, there are some other galleries, off to one side. The other Sophies are in there. I've looked, and each of them has a small grey key just like mine. None of them work, of course. I've tried them all, one by one, many times, over the days.

"I didn't realize how much like you he was," I say. "If you could talk to me, I wonder if you'd tell the same story, or whether it would be different. How different would it be? Were you really the way he told me you were?" The other Sophies are lined up quite neatly, although none of them look as if they were asleep, like Sophie does. I suppose Mattie comes back, eventually, to make sure everything is neat and tidy, the way it ought to be.

I take out the key again, turn it between my fingers. I feel slightly light-headed. It's not surprising, really. I have been through an awful lot, when you think about it.

"Will you tell me your story, then?" I say. "The true story? The real one?"

*That'll take a while*, Sophie says. I smile. She has a pretty voice, low and gentle.

"There's still enough time," I say.

© Jeremy Moeran

GUY BURT won the W. H. Smith Young Writers Award when he was twelve. He wrote *The Hole*, his first novel, when he was eighteen, and his second novel, *Sophie*, soon thereafter. He is also the author of *The Dandelion Clock*. Burt attended Oxford University and taught for three years at Eton. He lives in Oxford.

# Don't miss this compelling novel of psychological suspense by Guy Burt

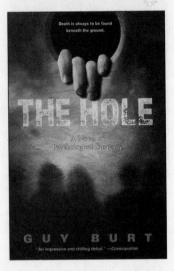

On a spring day in England, six teenagers venture to a neglected part of their school where there is a door to a small windowless cellar. Behind the door, the old stairs have rotted away. A boy unfurls a rope ladder and five descend into The Hole. The sixth closes the door, locks it from the outside, and walks calmly away. The plan is simple: They will spend three days locked in The Hole and emerge to become part of the greatest prank the school has ever seen. But something goes terribly wrong. No one is coming back to let them out . . . ever.

"Chilling . . . akin to *The Blair Witch Project* . . . The writing is remarkably assured. . . . A story about that most elemental of human fears, being buried alive."

—*The New York Times Book Review*

Published by Ballantine Books.
Available wherever books are sold.